In at the Kill

By E. X. Ferrars

In at the Kill

E. X. FERRARS

PUBLISHED FOR THE CRIME CLUB BY

DOUBLEDAY & COMPANY, INC.

GARDEN CITY, NEW YORK

1979

All of the characters in this book are fictitious, and
any resemblance to actual persons, living or dead, is
purely coincidental.

Library of Congress Cataloging in Publication Data

Ferrars, E. X.
In at the kill.

I. Title.
PZ3.B81742In 1979 [PR6003.R458]   823'.9'12
ISBN: 0-385-14913-1
Library of Congress Catalog Card Number 78-20025

In at the Kill

CHAPTER ONE

The second-class carriage was half empty. There was no reason why the sandy-haired man with the canvas zip-bag should have chosen to sit down facing Charlotte when there were so many other empty seats. She was afraid that he would turn out to be one of the people who like to talk in trains. She, herself, in the mood that she was in that day, was not one of them. As he pushed his bag into the luggage rack, took off his overcoat, rolled it into a bundle on the seat beside him and sat down, she turned a page of the paperback that she had bought at the Paddington bookstall and made it plain that she intended to read.

It did not put him off. "Miserable day," he said cheerfully.

"Yes," she agreed without looking up.

"The forecast said there'd be snow in the north."

"Did it?"

"Not that they often get it right, but it's cold enough." He had brought a couple of newspapers with him, but he laid them down on the table before him and showed no sign of wanting to read. "And as usual, when it's cold, something seems to have gone wrong with the heating in here. Have you noticed how that always happens? On a pleasant warm day they boil you alive, but as soon as the temperature drops, they make a point of turning all the heat off. Luckily, I'm not going far, only to Mattingley. That's just about an hour and a quarter from here. Do you know Mattingley?"

"Slightly," she said.

"Then d'you happen to know about the hotels there? Is there anything tolerable?"

"I'm sorry, I don't know. I've only been there once, and I didn't stay overnight."

"Tolerable but not too expensive," he went on. "That's a lot to ask these days, isn't it? Everything costs the earth. I suppose you aren't going there yourself?"

"As a matter of fact, I am." She might have denied it. It might have been sensible to do so. But she was not very good at lying; and, besides, they'd both be getting off at the same station. Giving up her attempt to read, however, she took her first real look at the man.

He was about thirty, thin and not very tall, with a pale face with thin, sharp undistinguished features, light blue eyes and sandy hair that he wore rather shorter than the fashion of the moment. He was wearing a light grey suit that had certainly not cost much, a grey-and-white-striped shirt and a dark blue tie with an unobtrusive red pattern on it. She had seen people like him so often that she had a feeling that if she were to look down at her book again she would immediately forget what he looked like.

Yet suddenly Charlotte felt convinced that she had seen him before. But the feeling came and went, leaving her sure that he had seemed familiar for that moment only because he was so entirely commonplace. If she looked out at the station platform, she thought, she would see dozens of him going by.

"You're visiting friends, I expect," he said.

"No," she answered.

"No? It's just that I can't think of any other reason for going to a place like Mattingley on a cold Saturday afternoon in December, unless, like me, you've got business there. I've a job to do that may keep me there a few days, otherwise you wouldn't get me away from my own fireside. For one thing, having to be away at the week-end, I'll miss the kids. I see little enough of them as it is, with them generally being in bed by the time I get home, the younger ones anyway, and the older ones spending their evenings doing homework. So the week-end's really the only time I get to see anything of them. But you can't always pick and choose what you have to do."

"You've got children?" she said, somehow surprised. He did not strike her as looking like a family man. "How many?"

He hesitated, as if he were mentally counting on his fingers.

"Five," he answered.

In another moment, she felt, he would be showing her their photographs.

But she was wrong. He only gave her a faintly mocking grin, as if he felt that he was one up on her, having produced such a brood when she, if the absence of a wedding-ring on her finger was anything to go by, had so far produced none.

Charlotte, however, who was actually not very fond of children, felt that this put her one up on him. To have reached the age of twenty-four without becoming loaded with the responsibility of a family had taken some determination. It was only very occasionally that she felt any regrets at time slipping by without bringing her a husband or children.

In one such mood, only recently, she had gone so far as to accept an offer of marriage, only to cancel it next day in a panic at committing herself so deeply, and although this had put an end to what had been a very comfortable relationship and had left her, for the time being, rather lonely, she had not felt in the least tempted to change her mind again.

It was not the only time that she had come near to marriage. She was not a beauty by any means, yet she had been found attractive by a fair number of men, which puzzled her, for she was inclined to think of herself as plain and too straight up and down to be in the least seductive, and she knew that she was incapable of dressing well or making the most of herself.

Today she was wearing a sheepskin jacket over a heavy black sweater and dark green slacks. She was small and slight, though surprisingly strongly built, and had a rosy face, wide at the temples, with high cheekbones and a pointed chin. It seemed a friendly face at first sight, but there was a detachment in her gaze that could be chilling once you had recognized it in her soft, golden-brown eyes. Her hair was brown, darker than her eyes, and she had dark, level, rather formidable eyebrows.

At present she lived by herself in a flat in Maida Vale, and for the last two years had been doing research for a retired general who had been writing the history of his family. But the general had recently died, and although Charlotte had grieved for the old man, who had been kind and generous even if the work that she had been doing for him had been appallingly dull, to be free at the moment happened to suit her rather well. There were concerns of hers that needed attention. Serious attention. That simply had to be faced.

The carriage was filling up. A stout woman with a flushed, flustered face, a bulging shopping bag and some miscellaneous parcels, which she kept counting to make sure that she had not left any of them behind, dumped herself in the seat beside Charlotte and at once began to tell her and the man with sandy hair about the travail of a day's shopping in London. She was going to Mattingley too. In fact, she told them, she lived there. Yet the man did not ask her for advice about hotels, which no doubt she could have given him, but picking up one of his newspapers, began to study the sports page.

It gave Charlotte a chance to go back to her paperback, a collection of ghost stories, not really the best possible reading for a railway journey, but it had been the best thing that she had been able to find in a hurry at the station. A few minutes later the train began to move, passing from the lights of the station into the dusk of the world outside, dusk speckled with the shining points of street lamps and that soon deepened into darkness. A flurry of rain struck the windows, desolate and wintry.

The stout woman soon slipped into a doze and when her head was nodding on her bosom and little snuffly sounds were coming from between her soft, parted lips, the sandy-haired man put his newspaper down again and remarked to Charlotte, "This isn't the time of year you'd choose for a holiday."

Charlotte read on.

He leant towards her. "I said, this isn't my idea of weather for a holiday."

"No," she agreed.

"Of course, it would be different if one could go abroad, Majorca or wherever. Even so, I prefer a summer holiday."

"So do I."

"You aren't going on holiday now, then?"

"Well, I shan't be working."

"So it *is* a holiday."

"Call it a break."

"A break between one job and the next, is that it? Don't tell me you're out of a job. That'd be bad these days."

Charlotte laid her book down on the table. "I'd far

sooner not tell you anything about my job or anything else. I can't think why you're asking me all these questions."

He smiled apologetically. "Sorry, it's a bad habit I have. I'm interested in people and mostly people like to chat. Of course, you have to start with the commonplace, boring things like the weather and foreign travel before you can get on to anything interesting, but you'd be surprised at the things I've been told on trains and buses and so on. Only a week ago a woman told me the whole inside story of her divorce, which never came out in court and which even her husband didn't know. It's the attraction, you see, of telling your troubles to someone you know you'll never meet again and who's sympathetic and glad to listen. You feel quite safe and you let yourself go."

"And what confidences do you contribute to these exchanges?" Charlotte asked. "Only your five children?"

"Oh no, my genuine interest, that's the main thing."

"Well, I'm afraid I've nothing interesting to tell you."

"Now there I'm sure you're wrong," he said. "As soon as I sat down opposite you, I said to myself, 'There's a very troubled person.'"

"Oh God," Charlotte said, "I believe you belong to one of those crazy religious groups who try to buttonhole you when you're busy and sell you salvation. Aren't we going to get around to my soul soon?"

"Not unless it's on your mind, though of course it's a very interesting subject."

"If you don't mind, I'd sooner just go on reading in peace."

"That's quite all right," he said. "You do that. I never intrude when I'm not welcome."

Wondering just what else he had been trying to do ever since he had got into the train, Charlotte picked up her book again and went on reading.

When the train stopped at Mattingley it was raining coldly and steadily. The stout woman woke with a start, assembled her parcels and lumbered off towards the door. Charlotte stood up, buttoned her jacket and stooped to pull her suitcase out from behind her seat.

The sandy-haired man watched her for a moment, then said, "Let me help."

She stood aside so that he could reach the case.

"Heavy," he remarked. "Well, if you'll carry my bag, I'll do my best with this. You won't find a porter anywhere."

"That's very kind of you," she said, grateful, but making it plain she was keeping her distance. She took his canvas bag from him while he dragged her case into the gangway.

"Someone meeting you, or d'you want a taxi?" he asked.

"A taxi, if there is such a thing," she said.

"Well, we'll see."

He set off towards the door with Charlotte following him.

There were several taxis waiting in the rank outside the station. He put the case into the nearest cab and held the door open for Charlotte to climb in.

"Where d'you want to go?" he asked.

This was something that she could have told the driver herself. But in view of the man's helpfulness with her case, she did not want to be discourteous.

"Beech Cottage, Brickett's Farm," she said.

He repeated this to the driver, who gave a grunt to indicate that he knew the place. The sandy-haired man shut the door, and stood there looking after her as the taxi drove off. He had still not moved when the taxi swung out of sight, even though his hair was plastered to his head by the rain and his pale face gleamed with moisture. So of course he had recognized her. He had known all along who she was. Really that had been obvious from the start.

The taxi drove through the lighted streets of the town, then out into the darkness of country lanes. The headlights slid across high, bare hedges with branches shiny with dampness. The drive took about twenty minutes. When the taxi stopped at a gate in a high beech hedge, the driver helped Charlotte with her suitcase as far as the front door of the cottage and while his headlights still lit up the front of it, she found the key in her handbag and pushed it into the lock. As the taxi drove on to the entrance to a driveway a little further on down the lane, where it could turn, and started back to Mattingley, she opened the cottage door.

She had been here only once, a week ago, when she had arranged to rent it furnished for a month. It had originally been a farm labourer's cottage, in the days when Brickett's Farm had still been a farm and not a rich man's country house. It took her a moment, groping beside the door, to find the light-switch, but the room was not entirely dark. There was a dim red light in it, as well as an unexpected warmth. Someone had been in and turned on the electric fire.

There was a thoughtfulness in this that surprised her. Mr. Frensham, the man who lived in the old farmhouse and who had shown her over the cottage the Saturday before, had not struck her as the kind who was likely to be much concerned about the comfort of his tenants. He had wanted only to close the deal with her as quickly as possible and be rid of her.

This had made her feel baulked. She was impatient to learn as much as she could about him as quickly as she could, but except for what she had known about him already, that he was a remarkably handsome man of about forty, black-haired, blue-eyed, with an air of cool arrogance that had verged on discourtesy, she had learnt nothing of interest about him. Unless it had been significant that her name had apparently meant nothing to him. Hadn't that been strange?

However, he had mentioned a housekeeper he had, Miss Sharples, and it was probably she, Charlotte thought, who had come to switch on the welcoming fire. Someone had also put a bottle of milk, some eggs, a loaf of bread and a half pound of butter on the kitchen table, and a vase with a few sprigs of winter jasmine in it on the small dining table in the sitting-room.

There were only the sitting-room and the kitchen on the ground floor, their walls painted white and with dark red curtains at their small windows. The chairs were wicker and the table with the jasmine on it had metal legs and a plastic top of imitation rosewood. There was a writing-table in one corner and a bookcase with a few old paperbacks in it in another. There was nothing to which the people who came and went here could do much damage. And on the whole the bareness and simplicity of the place appealed to Charlotte. It would be very easy to keep clean, and it was totally impersonal. That was something that she valued very much just then when too many unwelcome things had intruded into her private life.

A door in the sitting-room, which looked like that of a cupboard, opened on to a steep staircase to the floor above, where there were two small bedrooms, one leading out of the other, and a rather primitive bathroom. The modernizing of the cottage, such as had been done, had been carried out crudely and cheaply. But at least there was an electric cooking stove in the kitchen, a refrigerator and an immersion heater for the hot water. Charlotte hung up her jacket on a peg in the kitchen, put the milk, butter and eggs in the refrigerator, then took her suitcase upstairs and unpacked it. She had not brought many clothes, but she had brought a packet of tea, a tin of ham, a tin of stewed steak

and vegetables, some biscuits, some cheese and some toma-
toes. Enough, she had thought, to see her through until
Monday, when she could go shopping locally. With the
supplies that had been provided by Miss Sharples there was
more than enough. Stowing her clothes in the chest of
drawers in the bigger bedroom, she brought her provisions
downstairs and put on the kettle for a cup of tea.

She drank the tea sitting close to the shining bars of the
electric fire. As the cold of the winter evening thawed out of
her, it occurred to her that this was one of the first peaceful
moments that she had experienced for some weeks. Even if
she was scared of what lay ahead of her, there was a sense
of achievement in simply having arrived at this place that
was very satisfying. She had planned and acted, and now
she was here. What was to happen next was anybody's
guess, but for the moment she could simply sit back, relax,
dream, give herself a few days to enjoy the quiet of it, and
sleep a great deal, if she was lucky. Better, she hoped, than
she had been sleeping recently.

Yet after relaxing for only a few minutes, she began to
feel restless, wanting to be doing something. That she nearly
always needed to be doing something and was capable of
enjoying peace only in very small doses was something that
had afflicted her a great deal lately. She tried to resist it, but
without much success. This evening, as soon as she had
finished her tea, she put on her jacket again, took a torch
she had brought with her out of her handbag and set out
into the darkness. She wanted to see the man Frensham
again as soon as possible and thought to herself, why wait?

The rain had almost stopped, but the ground was sodden
and water soon leaked into her shoes. She found her way to
the entrance to the drive where the taxi had turned, found
gates there, went in and started up the drive. As soon as she
turned into it she could see the lights of the big house

ahead. It was too dark for her to see anything but its outline, but from her visit last week she remembered that it was
an old house, ivy-grown, with weathered tiles and casement
windows, the kind of house that looks unostentatious and
yet at the same time gives an impression of great luxury.
There was a car standing in front of it, a small, white,
rather battered Renault. Charlotte made her way round it,
went up to the front door and was just going to ring the bell
when she saw that the door was open.

But even though the door was open, the normal thing to
do was to ring the bell. She heard it peal shrilly inside, but
no one came to answer it. The door was only a few inches
open, but there was light inside. She rang again and this
time, after a moment, heard footsteps coming to the door,
almost running. The door was pulled open by a woman who
stood still, peering into the darkness.

"Who is it?" she asked sharply. "What d'you want?"

"I'm Charlotte Cambrey," Charlotte answered. "I've just
moved into Beech Cottage. Are you Miss Sharples?"

"Who? Oh—oh yes, I'm Miss Sharples."

The woman had opened the door only a little way and
with the light behind her it was difficult for Charlotte to
make out much of her features, but she was not what Charlotte had expected of the housekeeper. For one thing, she
was young. It was easy to tell that from her slender outline
and the way that she held herself, even though her face was
in shadow.

"I came to thank you for getting in the milk and things,"
Charlotte said, "and for turning on the fire. It was nice to
come into a warm house. And for the jasmine too. That was
specially nice."

"You needn't have bothered." The woman's voice was
deep, with the sort of huskiness that can sound attractive,
but which at the moment sounded nervous and impatient.

"And I brought the rent," Charlotte went on. "I arranged with Mr. Frensham I'd pay weekly in advance."

"There's no hurry about it," the woman said. "Any time will do."

"But I'd like to settle up if I can," Charlotte insisted. "And there are one or two things I'd like to ask you."

"Ask me?" the woman said abruptly. The thought seemed to startle her. "What d'you mean?"

"Well, where the nearest shop is and that sort of thing. It would help a lot."

"Oh—oh, I see. Yes." The woman sounded relieved. At last she stepped back, opening the door wider. "Come in, then. There's a shop in the village where you can get most things—that's only about a quarter of a mile further on along the road—and some of the Mattingley shops deliver here. The Mattingley shops are quite good. Have you a car?"

"No," Charlotte answered.

"Well, there's a reasonable bus service. There's a bus once an hour and the bus-stop's almost opposite the gates here."

Seen in the light of the hall, the reason for the woman's impatience was obvious. She was dressed to go out in a grey tweed coat with a high fox collar, gloves and a handbag tucked under her arm. Her head was bare. She had smooth, very pale blonde hair which was drawn straight back from her face and coiled up at the back of her head. She had light grey eyes with long, dark lashes, the sort of eyes that might have been beautiful if they had not had a glassy, almost unseeing look. Her age was about thirty. Her oval face was abnormally, almost frighteningly pale and though the lipstick that she was wearing was a light-coloured one, it had the look of a wound against that glaring pallor.

"Is Mr. Frensham in?" Charlotte asked. "I don't want to keep you if you're going out. I could give him the rent."

She was taking in her surroundings as she spoke, a small, square hall with a low ceiling, striped with dark rafters, walls of a soft green, a dark green carpet, one heavily carved chair, an oak chest with linenfold panels, several doors, all closed, and a wide, straight staircase, carpeted in the same green as the hall. There was something about the staircase that puzzled her. What looked like a pair of rails had been laid down one side of it. She could not think what their purpose was.

"No, he's out," Miss Sharples said. "You can give me the money if you want to, though, as I said, it doesn't really matter."

Charlotte took seven five pound notes out of her handbag and held them out.

Miss Sharples took them and laid them down carelessly on the oak chest.

"Anything else you want?" she asked, looking at Charlotte, obviously expecting her to leave.

Something made Charlotte say, "If you wouldn't mind giving me a receipt . . ."

A quick frown appeared on the other woman's smooth forehead. All of a sudden she looked so exasperated that she might have been about to lose her temper completely. But she controlled it, the frown disappeared, her face became once more an expressionless mask and she said in her low, harsh voice, "Of course. Just a minute."

Taking the money that Charlotte had given her, she opened one of the closed doors and disappeared through it.

While she was gone Charlotte moved nearer to the staircase and looked at the rails down the side of it. At the top of the stairs, she saw, a kind of chair was attached to them. She realized now what it was. It was an electric chair-lift, of a kind which she had seen in advertisements but had never seen at first hand. It meant that someone in the house was an invalid, perhaps a heart-case or a severe arthritic. She wondered who it was. Mr. Frensham had made no mention of anyone living in the house with him except Miss Sharples. For whom the word housekeeper was perhaps a euphemism.

Miss Sharples came back to the hall in a moment, holding a pad of paper and a ballpoint pen. Sitting down on the oak chest, she put the pad on her knee and began to take off her gloves so that she could write. But she had her first glove barely half off when she jerked it on again and took off only the other. She had not been so quick about it, however, that Charlotte had not had the chance to see the wedding-ring on her finger. An inappropriate thing for someone who called herself Miss Sharples to wear.

"What's the date?" the woman asked. "December the twelfth, isn't it? And what did you say your name was?"

"Cambrey," Charlotte answered. "Charlotte Cambrey."

It seemed strange that someone who had taken the trouble to switch on her fire in the cottage and put jasmine in a vase should not know her name.

"Oh, yes." Miss Sharples wrote quickly, tore the page from the pad and held it out. "Will that do?"

In a sloping, rather spidery writing, she had written, "December 12th, received from Miss C. Cambrey £35.00, one week's rent for Beech Cottage. E. Sharples."

"Yes, thank you," Charlotte said. "And thank you for your help. But I owe you something too for the milk and the other things. How much did they come to?"

"Oh, don't bother about them. I can't remember just how much it was. Are you thinking of staying long?"

"I've taken the cottage for a month."

"What are you going to do with yourself?"

"Rest, mainly. I haven't been very well."

"Oh, I'm sorry." Miss Sharples seemed suddenly to want to erase the impression of her impatience, but it was obviously an effort. "You'll certainly be able to rest here. It's very quiet. And there's a nice doctor in the village, if you want one. Dr. Maynard."

"Oh, I hope it won't come to that."

"You'll probably meet him anyhow. The neighbours are friendly." Miss Sharples stood up, pulling on the glove that she had taken off. "But perhaps you don't want that."

"I haven't really thought about it."

"Well, anything I can do, just let me know." She smiled. But the stretching of her lips in the white oval of her face was more of a grimace than anything.

Charlotte thanked her again and turned to the door.

It was not left open now when she went out by it, but was closed behind her with a quick slam. Yet she was only halfway down the drive when the white Renault came roaring past her, sending a swish of water from a puddle over her ankles and swinging out into the road without the driver, it seemed to Charlotte, pausing even for a moment to see if other traffic was coming from either direction. The car turned towards Mattingley. It and its lights had disappeared before she reached the end of the drive.

Walking on, she wondered if Miss Sharples had just deserted Mr. Frensham permanently and gone to meet a newly acquired husband, hence the wedding-ring, or if it was just a week-end wedding-ring, brought into use only now and then. But one strange thing was certain, and that was that the woman had been very scared of something. The tension, the white face and unseeing eyes had been those of someone suffering from some intense fear.

Back in the cottage, Charlotte took off her damp shoes, put on a pair of bedroom slippers and settled down in one of the wicker chairs by the fire. She had begun to feel very tired. Presently, she thought, she would open the tin of stewed steak and heat it up and make some more tea, but there was no need to hurry about it. Yet, in fact, she did not sit by the fire for long. The restlessness that plagued her so much these days soon made her get up and walk over to the bookcase to see what sort of books her predecessor had left behind. It turned out that the paperbacks left behind on the shelves were all romances, and she preferred her ghost stories to that, though she would soon have finished them. It was a pity that there was neither television nor radio in the cottage. She seemed to need something this evening to break the stillness of the little room. If she had thought more clearly when she was packing, she could easily have brought her transistor. Perhaps, she thought, it would be a good idea to go into Mattingley on Monday morning and hire a television for a month. Yes, she would do that. Meanwhile, she might as well cook her supper. Going into the kitchen, she opened the tin of steak and poured the contents into a saucepan.

When it was heated up, she tipped the not very appetizing stew onto a plate, cut a slice from the loaf that Miss Sharples had left for her, found a knife and fork in a drawer and returned to the sitting-room. She had just begun to eat when she was startled by the squeak of the gate, the sound of stumbling footsteps outside her door and then a frenzied pounding on it with the door-knocker.

For a moment she did not move. One of the things that she had decided when she took the cottage, realizing how isolated she would be there, was that she must not open the door at night to any unknown visitor. But the pounding with the door-knocker was repeated, and a woman's voice cried out, "Miss Cambrey! Miss Cambrey, are you there? Oh, do let me in!"

Putting down her plate of stew, Charlotte went to the door and opened it.

A small, round woman stood there, clothed in a coat of brilliant blue and a rakishly tilted blue felt hat that showed grey elf-locks under it. Her high-heeled shoes and her stockings were splashed with mud. Her face was small, soft, doughey and frantic.

"Miss Cambrey—you *are* Miss Cambrey, aren't you?" The woman came stumbling forward into the room. "Oh, thank God you're here, dear. Just to have *someone* here . . . I don't know what to do, you see. I'm not clever at things like this. I lose my head. 'Emily,' Mr. Frensham always said to me, 'you must keep calm. You're a wonderful woman, but you lose your head at every little thing that goes wrong.' That's what he said to me, he really did. 'You're a wonderful woman,' he said. That's what he thought of me. And now he's gone. Oh dear, oh dear!"

She dropped into a chair and began to sob wildly.

Charlotte, feeling bewildered and helpless, put a hand on her shoulder and patted it awkwardly.

"Who are you?" she asked. "What's happened?"

"Why, I'm Miss Sharples, dear, Mr. Frensham's house-keeper." The little woman looked up at Charlotte through her streaming tears. "I only got home a few minutes ago—it's my afternoon off, I've been into Mattingley to my sister's—and I came in and found him. Dead, Miss Cambrey. Cold and dead. He's lying there in the drawing-room with half his head blown off and blood and everything all over the carpet. Oh, it's a terrible sight. I was frightened out of my wits. I can't stand looking at things like that. And the lift's gone wrong and Mrs. Frensham can't get downstairs and she's just standing up there at the top, shouting at me to get an electrician. I ask you, Mr. Frensham's lying there murdered and Mrs. Frensham goes on and on shouting at me to get an electrician. I know there are people I ought to get, but not an electrician, not just now, would you say that? Only I can't seem to think properly. I don't know what to do. So I came to you. I thought, she's young and she'll keep her head and she'll be clever with the telephone. Young people are all clever with the telephone, they'll talk on it for hours. But I can't seem to follow what anyone says. So you'll come up to the house with me now, won't you, dear, and telephone the police, because that's what I'm sure we ought to do, isn't that right? And the doctor too. We've got to get them as soon as possible."

CHAPTER TWO

The first thought that came into Charlotte's mind, but which came and went so swiftly that she was hardly aware of it, was that if Edgar Frensham was dead, she might as well go straight back to London.

Her next thought was a wish that it had occurred to her to bring a bottle of whisky in her suitcase. The little woman had begun to shake. She shook so violently that the chair she was sitting in began an eery creaking. Whisky might have helped. But Charlotte very seldom drank when she was alone, and she had not expected visitors.

It was also unfortunate that there was no telephone in the cottage from which she could have called the police and the doctor without delay.

Fetching her jacket, changing her shoes once more and picking up her torch, she said, "All right, let's go. But do you think you can manage it? You wouldn't sooner just rest here?"

"No, dear, I'm all right, quite all right," the little woman said. "It's just the shock, you know, upsetting me. Coming home—can you imagine it?—expecting to get the dinner and finding . . ." She choked on the words. Getting to her feet, she panted slightly. "And then the trouble with the lift, which has never gone wrong before, and her shouting at me and me not knowing what to say. I went upstairs to her and I said, 'Something terrible's happened, dear,' I said. 'I think you should go back and lie down till I can get Dr. Maynard.' I hadn't the courage, you see, to tell her what had really happened, and she just went on and on about the lift. She's like that, she does go on and on about things and says terrible things to me, though of course she doesn't mean them. And I did try to phone Dr. Maynard, but I only got his answering service, telling me where to ring him and that always makes me feel nervous. It feels so queer hearing that voice telling you what to do and you can't answer back or ask any questions. So then I thought of coming to you. I hope you don't mind, dear. It seemed the best thing to do."

Charlotte had taken her arm, led her to the door and opened it.

"Mrs. Frensham is his wife, is she?" she asked as they started out into the darkness. "I didn't know he had one."

"No, dear, she's his stepmother," Miss Sharples answered. "Quite an old lady. Very rich. She owns the house and the cottages and all. But they're very fond of each other, just like a real mother and son. He looks after the estate for her, and whatever you can say against him, he's been ever so good to her since she had her stroke and got paralyzed down one side. He thought of putting the lift in for her. Without it she couldn't hardly manage the stairs."

With the beam of the torch wavering ahead of them, they made for the gates of the drive.

"Are there some more cottages, then?" Charlotte asked.

"Yes, dear, this was quite a big farm once, though Mrs. Frensham's father sold off most of the land. But there were several cottages for the farm labourers, and they've all been modernized, just like yours, and they're rented out, some for just a few weeks and some with quite long leases, like Miss Bird's. She must have been here all of two years. And Mr. Havershaw must have been here a year now and Mrs. Neville must have been three months at least. Then there are Mr. and Mrs. Grainger, who just took theirs for three months too. Of course, I know them all better than I do you, so perhaps I ought to have gone to one of them, but I came to you because you're nearest."

Wobbling on her high heels, she was having difficulty dodging the puddles picked out by the light of the torch.

"I'd such a nice day too," she went on. "My sister's son and his wife were there and we had a lovely tea, and then Tom—that's my nephew—drove me home and if only he'd come in with me he could have managed everything, because he's ever such a practical young man. He might even have put the lift right. He's very clever with the electricity. But he just put me down at the door and drove away again, because, after all, how could he know what had happened?"

"Is there any other Miss Sharples besides yourself?" Charlotte asked. "A niece or a cousin or anything?"

"No, dear, there's just me. My sister's name is Mrs. Cartwright, and that's Tom's name too, of course. Why, what made you ask?"

"I just wondered," Charlotte said.

They turned in at the gates of the drive. It seemed to have grown colder than it had been earlier in the evening, though the sky was clearing. A few stars shone between heavy banks of cloud. But the air still smelt of wet earth and grass and there was a quiet drip, drip among the bushes as raindrops slithered down their branches. The house had even more lights shining in its windows than when Charlotte had come to it last. It looked as if it had been lit up for a party.

Miss Sharples unlocked the front door, then stood back nervously to make sure that Charlotte went in before her.

A shrill voice called out, "Who's there?"

"It's me, dear—Emily," Miss Sharples answered, going to the foot of the stairs and looking up.

Charlotte also looked up and saw the chair attached to

the rails of the lift still at the upper landing, as she had seen it before, but there was no one standing beside it.

"Who's that you've got with you?" the voice demanded.

It came from one of the doors in the hall, which had been closed when Charlotte had been here before, but which now stood open.

Miss Sharples rushed to the door, then abruptly stood still, as if she had run into an invisible barrier.

"Oh, I can't go in there," she said in a trembling voice. "Not again. No, I couldn't do that." Then raising her voice, she said, "What are you doing in there, Mrs. Frensham, dear? How did you get downstairs?"

"On my bottom," the voice answered. "I can still do it, though it takes time. I'm not quite helpless. Where have you been, you silly woman, leaving me all alone?"

"Just to get help. I didn't think you'd come downstairs." Miss Sharples was making frantic gestures to Charlotte to advance to the doorway. "This is Miss Cambrey, who's taken Beech Cottage. She's come to help us call the police and all."

Charlotte went to the door. Her heart suddenly started to thud painfully. She had seen death a number of times, but never violent death, and although she was to some extent prepared for what she would see, an atavistic dread of having to look at it gave her a shock of fear that her legs were going to crumple under her.

This did not show outwardly. Except that her eyes opened wider than usual and seemed to darken in colour as she took in the scene before her, she appeared quite self-possessed. This was her normal reaction at first to catastrophe, an apparent calm, which in its way could be useful, though she knew that she would have to pay for it heavily later.

The room was a square one with a low ceiling, like the

hall. There was a big old fireplace in which logs had been laid, but not set alight. Yet the room was very warm, heated by two long radiators. There was rather too much furniture in it, mostly of dark polished mahogany, and there were several portraits on the walls of stiff-looking ladies and gentlemen in the caps and wigs of the eighteenth century. The carpet was ivory-coloured and the curtains, which had not been drawn, were of dull pink velvet. Every light in the room had been turned on. The glare of them on the blood on the ivory carpet gave it an obscene sort of radiance, although it was already beginning to darken.

The man whose blood it was lay sprawled in the middle of the room with his arms flung out, one side of his face hidden in the carpet, the rest of it a mess of brains and shattered bone. Sitting in a chair near him, looking steadily down at him with an air of thoughtful curiosity, was a very old woman.

She looked as if she must be at least ninety. She was probably tall, but she was so thin and she sat in so crouched a position that she seemed shrunken to a mere dried-up wisp of humanity. With each hand, deformed by arthritis, she held an aluminum crutch. She was wearing a quilted purple dressing-gown and sparkling diamond ear-rings in her ears. Her face was long, her nose and chin sharply pointed, her skin sallow and deeply wrinkled. All the life in her face was in her eyes, dark as prunes and large and fierce. She seemed reluctant to withdraw them from keeping watch on the dead man on the floor, as if he might take it into his head to do something disturbing if she glanced away from him for a moment.

However, looking up at Charlotte, she said, "You can go away. You'll be no bloody use here. I've called Dr. Maynard and he's calling the police. They'll be here soon."

Charlotte, who was feeling sick and wanted to get out of

the room as quickly as she could, replied, "I'll go, if you like. But there's something I can tell the police that I think they ought to know."

"Oh, there is, is there? You're one of those. Busybodies. Mad about sensation. Poking their bloody noses in where they aren't wanted. How can you possibly have anything to tell the police? Did you know my stepson?"

"I've only spoken to him once, when he was showing me the cottage," Charlotte answered.

"There you are, then. So you can go home. We're quite capable of coping with things without your interference. You're much too young to be any use. I wonder what Edgar was thinking of, letting a cottage to someone as young as you."

"Now, dear, is that a nice way to talk to the young lady?" Miss Sharples said. She had advanced a little way into the room, but was keeping her eyes away from the dead man. "She only came because I went and asked her to. I never thought you'd manage to get downstairs without the lift, and I didn't like to tell you what had happened and you know I'm not good on the telephone. So I went and got Miss Cambrey, and it's very kind of her to have come. Now don't go on sitting there. It doesn't look quite nice. It's morbid. Come into the study and I'll get you a glass of whisky. That's what you'd like, isn't it? Come along now."

She grasped Mrs. Frensham by the arm to help her to her feet.

"Leave me alone, leave me alone!" the old woman shouted at her, hammering the ground with one of her crutches. "I can manage by myself. Can't you understand I'm not a bloody cripple yet?" She looked up at Charlotte again. "D'you know anything about electricity?"

"A little," Charlotte said.

"Then go and look in the cupboard under the stairs.

That's where all the fuses and switches are. See if you can find what went wrong with my lift. Because it was put out of order on purpose, that's obvious, so that I shouldn't come down and catch them killing Edgar. Not that they need have troubled. I had a long sleep this afternoon and didn't wake up till I heard Emily rushing round downstairs as if she was demented. Whoever they were, I didn't hear a thing. If I'd come down earlier, I suppose they'd have knocked me off too, and no loss to anyone if they had. In the state I'm in, I'm just a burden to everyone, including myself, and there'd be some point in killing me, because I've money to leave a few people. People who'll be very happy when I die." She gave a gruesome sort of chuckle.

"Now come along, do," Miss Sharples said, once more grasping one of Mrs. Frensham's arms and beginning to haul her to her feet with surprising strength. The old woman accepted her help indifferently this time, as if she had never protested about it before. "Miss Cambrey will look in the cupboard and I'll get you a nice glass of whisky, and I'm sure Dr. Maynard will be here any minute."

Once on her feet, Mrs. Frensham balanced herself on her crutches and began to limp lopsidedly towards the door.

"You'd better get this girl a glass of whisky too," she said. "You can see she needs it. No stamina. None of the young have any stamina nowadays. Bloody weaklings."

Beginning to wish that in the days when Mrs. Frensham's favourite adjective had still been shocking, she had troubled to enlarge her vocabulary, Charlotte went to the cupboard under the stairs, opened it and peered in.

She saw a formidable array of fuses and switches. One switch beside the door, which she pressed experimentally, lit up a bulb that hung from the top of the cupboard, so that she could at least see what else there was inside it. A number of switches were labelled with small inked labels, main switch, bell, lights, heaters. There was one labelled lift. All the other switches had been pressed down, which presumably meant that they were on, but the one marked lift was pressed upwards.

Without touching it, Charlotte turned off the light in the cupboard, closed the door and went to the room which Mrs. Frensham, who had made her way very slowly across the hall, was just entering. It was a small room with a large, bleached, Scandinavian-looking desk and chair, two green metal filing cabinets, a safe, two oddly shaped armchairs made of plastic and steel tubing, of the kind that have no back legs and make you look as if you are sitting on air, some luridly coloured abstract paintings, a polished wood-block floor and scarlet curtains, which Miss Sharples was just drawing. Charlotte noticed that the money that she had given the blonde woman was on the desk.

"I hate this room," Mrs. Frensham said as she lowered herself cautiously on to one of the plastic chairs. "What did he want an office for? The amount of business he had to do, he could have kept all the papers in that nice old bureau I gave him." She looked round at Charlotte. "Have you found out what's wrong with the lift?"

"As far as I can see, someone turned it off at the main switch that controls it, that's all," Charlotte answered.

"Have you turned it on again?"

"No, I thought the police would want it left as it was."

"I suppose that's sense." But it was said grudgingly, while the fierce old black eyes studied Charlotte's face. It seemed to her that Mrs. Frensham was in a state of smouldering anger, so far showing no signs of grief at her stepson's death. She seemed outraged at the way that it had intruded into her own life, but not shocked or filled with sorrow.

A bell rang.

"That'll be Ralph Maynard," she said. "Let him in, Emily."

But Miss Sharples had just disappeared, probably to fetch the whisky that she had promised Mrs. Frensham.

"I'll go," Charlotte said and went out to the front door and opened it.

A man of about fifty stood there, wearing a tweed overcoat and a felt hat. As he took his hat off, it showed a head nearly bald with a little dark hair plastered across it. He had a comfortable face, round, plump and friendly, with small grey eyes which looked as if normally they would have held a twinkle, but which now were full of grave concern. Behind him in the drive was a grey Jaguar.

"I'm Dr. Maynard," he said. "Mrs. Frensham sent for me."

"I'm Charlotte Cambrey," Charlotte replied. "I've come to stay in Beech Cottage. Miss Sharples brought me here to help."

"Where is she?"

"Miss Sharples?"

"No, no, Mrs. Frensham."

He had said she, not he. It was the old woman whom he wanted to see, not the corpse.

Coming into the hall, he took off his overcoat and laid it and his hat down on the carved oak chair, doing it with an air of familiarity, as if he were a regular visitor here. Then he looked questioningly at Charlotte.

She led him into the room where Mrs. Frensham was sitting. She held out a hand to him. Bending over it, he pressed it gently.

"This is a terrible thing to have happened," he said. "Incredible."

She let her hand linger in his, giving him an almost flirtatious little smile.

"Oh, not really incredible," she said. "Such things are always happening nowadays. One keeps reading about them. It's merely that one doesn't expect them to happen to anyone one knows."

"It was theft then, was it? Someone broke in and Edgar interrupted them."

"I really don't know. We haven't got around to checking the silver yet. But it looks as if whoever it was knew his way about the house, because he turned off the main switch of my lift, so that I couldn't get downstairs. Actually I did get down, but I did it sitting down and sliding from step to step, and of course that hurt like the devil and took me a long time, and he'd have heard me coming, so he'd have had lots of time to get away, if he'd still been here, which he wasn't."

"So you don't know when it happened."

"No."

"You didn't hear anything?"

"No, I was asleep."

"Didn't Miss Sharples hear anything?"

"Saturday's her afternoon off. She'd gone into Mattingley to see her sister."

"Another thing that makes it look as if whoever it was knew the ways of the household, though of course he may simply have been watching for some time, or picked up some gossip in the village. A good many people must have known you'd had a lift installed and that you were nearly always at home. Now shall I—?" He broke off to give a little cough. "Shall I take a look at him?"

"Yes, would you, please, Ralph? It's in the drawing-room."

He gave a little tug to the front of his coat, smoothing it down as if he felt that it was only proper to present himself to the dead in a state of immaculate neatness, straightened his slightly bent shoulders and walked heavily out.

Only a moment after he had gone, Miss Sharples reappeared in the room, carrying a tray with bottles and glasses.

She had taken off her vivid blue coat and her high-heeled shoes, had combed her thin grey hair, put on pink, fur-lined bedroom slippers and was wearing a sober-looking grey jersey dress with a neat white collar.

She put the tray down on the writing-table.

"Now I know how you like yours, dear," she said to Mrs. Frensham and poured out a glass of neat whisky. "But how about you, Miss Cambrey? Soda? Water?"

"Water, please," Charlotte said.

"I've brought a glass for the doctor too," Miss Sharples said as she poured out Charlotte's drink. "And I had a nip of sherry myself out in the kitchen. I felt I needed something, and sherry suits me better than whisky. I like the cooking sherry best. That dry stuff you like always sets my teeth on edge. It really doesn't agree with me."

"God, how you talk," Mrs. Frensham said. "You'd better sit down," she added to Charlotte, "since you insist on staying. You too, Emily. The police are going to want to talk to all of us."

The police, Charlotte thought as she sat down, and the thing that she must remember to tell them. A glove that came half off, then was jerked back again, but not before she had caught a glimpse of a wedding-ring. She must certainly tell the police about that.

Dr. Maynard returned from the drawing-room. His face was blandly impersonal now, a purely professional face, kindly but detached. He asked for soda with his whisky, took it from Miss Sharples and drank most of it at a gulp.

"I haven't touched him, of course," he said, "except just to feel the temperature of his skin. I should say he's been dead for at least an hour, possibly more. But that's for Robart to say—the police surgeon from Mattingley. I can't say I'm experienced in these matters, but my impression is that he was shot and at fairly close quarters. Poor chap. Such a tough character. So strong and young for his age."

"You don't think by any chance it was suicide?" Mrs. Frensham asked.

"I didn't see any gun, though it might have fallen under him, I suppose. But I doubt if he'd have shot himself standing in the middle of the room, which is what he'd have had to do to fall where he is. He'd have been more likely to sit down at his desk in here and slump forward over it. More comfortable, somehow, to do it that way. But why d'you ask? Had he troubles that you know of, or has he ever said anything to you about suicide?"

"No," she said, sipping her whisky. "But I've been wondering about him lately. He's done some rather strange things. Not suicidal things, however. No, quite the reverse. He seemed very excitable, almost as if he were waiting for something. You knew him quite well, Ralph. You never noticed anything—well, strange?"

"Not a thing," he said.

She sighed. "I suppose one gets fanciful at my age. The fact is, I've sometimes felt afraid of him lately. How extraordinary things are."

The thought seemed to fill her with a mournful kind of satisfaction.

The doorbell rang again.

"That'll be the police," Dr. Maynard said, emptying his glass. "I'll let them in."

There were only two policemen at first, but then there were more, as well as photographers, setting off sudden flares of light, and finger-print men, who spread grey dust wherever they went, and an ambulance waiting in the drive, with two men sitting in it patiently, waiting to be told to remove the corpse and smoking cigarette after cigarette. There was also the police surgeon from Mattingley, Mr. Robart, who knew Dr. Maynard and chatted to him in the hall. The little that Charlotte overheard of their conversation appeared about the golf that they hoped to play next morning and what a pity it was that poor Frensham would not be able to join them. There hardly seemed to be room in the house for so many.

The man in charge of them all was Detective Superintendent Barr, a tall man, at least six foot three, with a great width of shoulder, so that in spite of a spare build, he looked far more powerful than anyone else there. He had a square, hard face, ruddy and smooth. His eyes were grey and singularly unblinking. After a while he established himself in the dining-room, a room with red walls and a red carpet, a great gilt-framed mirror over the fireplace and a crystal chandelier hanging above the centre of a circular walnut table. There he interviewed first Dr. Maynard, then Mrs. Frensham, then Miss Sharples and last Charlotte, while a sergeant sat at the table with him, taking notes.

Charlotte found that the time of waiting to be questioned passed very slowly. When her turn came, the Superintendent began by asking her name and address, then, leaning back in his chair and giving her a stare from those unblinking eyes which made her feel that he would remember every detail of her appearance till the day he died, he asked, "And just what are you doing here?"

"Here in this house, do you mean, or in Mattingley?" she asked.

"Let's take them both," he answered. "Mattingley first. What brought you here from London?"

"I wanted a rest," she said. "My job in London had just folded. My employer had died. And I thought I'd like a rest and a change before I looked for anything else. I'd saved some money, so I'd no need to hurry. And I happened to see an advertisement in a newspaper of a furnished cottage to let, so I telephoned the number they gave in the advertisement and talked to Mr. Frensham and arranged to come down to see the cottage last week. And I saw it and thought it was just what I wanted, and I arranged to take it for a month from today, and I arrived this afternoon."

"I see." He paused. "Not the best time of year for a holiday." He paused again. "Lonely and a bit too quiet I'd have thought for someone of your age."

"I don't mind that," she said. "Sometimes it's what one wants."

"About what time did you get here this afternoon?"

"I took the four-ten from Paddington, which gets to Mattingley about half past five, and I took a taxi from the station, which got me to the cottage I suppose about ten to six."

"Was Mr. Frensham there to let you in?"

"No, he gave me the key last week, as soon as I'd signed an informal sort of agreement. I let myself in."

"Didn't you see him at all this evening?"

"No, not until—well, until Miss Sharples brought me here this evening and I saw him . . ."

"Saw him dead. Ah yes." He nodded thoughtfully, taking some time before he went on. "She told us how she fetched you. So the only time you met him was that time last week."

"Yes." That was not precisely the truth, but was as much as she wanted to admit at present.

"Is that all you know about him? You spoke to him on the telephone in answer to an advertisement, you came down here, and he showed you the cottage and gave you the key to it, and that's all?"

"Yes." But she felt impelled to hurry on, "As a matter of

fact though, I came here earlier in the evening and a rather queer thing happened."

"You came here before Miss Sharples fetched you?"

"Yes."

"Why was that?"

"To say thank you to her for having bought me some milk and bread and so on and put them in the cottage and turned on the fire for me, so that it was nice and warm. Mr. Frensham had mentioned his housekeeper, and I thought she must be the person who'd thought of laying in supplies for me. And when I got here a woman who said she was Miss Sharples opened the door and let me in—that's to say, the door was open when I got here and there was a car in the drive—a white Renault—but this woman came to the door when I rang and when I told her who I was and why I'd come, she let me in and I gave her a week's rent and she gave me a receipt, which she signed E. Sharples. Only, you see, she wasn't Miss Sharples at all, she was someone quite different."

The Superintendent's unblinking expression did not alter, but he said, "That's very interesting. This receipt—have you got it?"

Charlotte searched in her handbag and brought out the receipt that the unknown woman had given her. He took it from her, read it carefully and laid it down on the table.

"You're certain this woman couldn't have been Miss Sharples?" he said. "There's no possibility you're mistaken?"

"Oh no, there was no resemblance between them whatever," she answered. "The woman was young—not more than thirty at the most—and very good-looking. She'd long, blonde hair, which she wore up, and she was wearing a very smart grey coat with a fox collar. And—oh, yes, she was wearing gloves and carrying a handbag, as if she was just going out. And it's strange about the gloves. When she wrote that receipt, she started to take them off, then suddenly she pulled the left one on again and took off only the right, but I'd already seen a wedding-ring she was wearing. And I thought it was odd that someone called Miss Sharples should be wearing a wedding-ring, but it never occurred to me then that she wasn't Miss Sharples at all."

"That's very interesting," Mr. Barr said again. "What time was this?"

"I think about half past six. I made myself some tea when I first got to the cottage, then came straight here."

"Did this woman say nothing about Mr. Frensham?"

"She said he was out and that she'd give him the money."

"Did nothing about her strike you as odd, apart from the wedding-ring?"

"Yes, I thought her manner was very odd," Charlotte said. "She was extremely pale and she seemed to be in a state of fearful nervousness, impatience. I wasn't sure what it was. But I got the impression she was very frightened of something."

"Didn't you see anything of Mrs. Frensham?"

"No, I think she must still have been asleep."

"And you didn't go into the drawing-room?"

"No, I stayed in the hall. All the doors were closed."

"So you can't tell if the murder had happened yet or not."

"No, but when I left and was about half-way down the drive, the white Renault came past me, being driven quite crazily, and it turned towards Mattingley."

"And the driver was the woman?"

"Yes."

Mr. Barr had a pause for thought, rubbing a finger along his smooth, heavy jawbone.

"Would you know her again, if you saw her?" he asked.

"I think so."

"What did she do with the money you gave her?"

"She took it into that room they call the office, the one with the safe in it. She went in there to fetch a pad of paper and a pen to write the receipt I'd asked for. The money's on the desk now."

"She went straight to that room? She didn't open any of the other doors first?"

"No."

"So she knew her way about the house. She knew that was the office. I wonder if she knew the combination of the safe. That safe's going to be a headache. It'll take an expert to open it. And Mrs. Frensham says she believes there's nothing in it, that there was never anything in the house in the way of valuables or documents that needed to be kept in a safe. She says her stepson had it put in just to make himself feel important. I suppose that's possible. How does that fit in with your own impression of him, Miss Cambrey? Did he seem to you a man with too little to do, except for small jobs like letting week-end cottages, but who liked to make a big impression?"

"I didn't think about it," Charlotte said, looking down so that she did not have to meet the steady stare of his eyes.

"Well, thank you for your help," he said. "You'll be staying at the cottage, will you?"

"I suppose so."

"A word of advice, don't open your door in the dark to strangers."

She took it as dismissal and stood up.

"Can I go back to the cottage now, or d'you want me to stay here?" she asked.

"No reason you shouldn't go home if you want to," he said. "But if you should think of leaving Mattingley, let us know."

She nodded and left the room.

She did not rejoin Mrs. Frensham and Miss Sharples in the office, but let herself out of the front door and set off down the drive. When she arrived at the cottage she found that the tinned stew which she had only just begun to eat when Miss Sharples came to her door had congealed on its plate and looked very unattractive. But she was hungrier than she had realized when she was in the big house, and after considering the matter for a moment, scraped what was left on the plate back into the saucepan, reheated it and hurriedly ate it. There were a great many problems at the back of her mind which she was trying not to think about, for she realized that she was too tired and too shocked to be able to think clearly. It would be better to wait till the morning. Heating some of the milk bought for her by Miss Sharples, she drank it, went to bed and slept deeply.

She woke only when she heard a noise of hammering, which sounded as if someone was trying to break into the cottage. Still only half-awake, she remembered that she should not open her door in the dark to strangers. But when she opened her eyes, she found that the room was filled with daylight, bright, white, frosty daylight, with a sparkle of sunshine in it. A glance at her watch told her that it was ten minutes past nine. The hammering was someone knocking on the front door.

Getting out of bed, she put on a dressing-gown and slippers, pulled a comb through her hair, went downstairs and opened the door.

A young man stood on the doorstep. He looked about twenty-five and was wearing a black-leather jacket and narrow, colourfully checked trousers. He was of medium height and had curly fair hair, which he wore half-way down to his shoulders, grey eyes and a fine scattering of freckles over his long, pale, slightly horse-like face. The smile with which he greeted Charlotte seemed to be full of an unusual number of large, uneven teeth. Yet it was a face with a good deal of charm and in a freakish way almost good-looking.

"I'm so sorry to trouble you so early," he said, "but I believe you saw the police yesterday and told them—oh, I'm forgetting, I'm Ian Havershaw and I live in Yew Tree Cottage. That's another of the cottages on the estate. We're neighbours. But—well, I believe you talked to the police and told them about a woman you saw up at Brickett's some time before anyone discovered Frensham's body, and I wondered—I wondered if you'd mind telling me about her too. You see, I think I know who she is."

"I'm just going to make some tea," Charlotte said. "Would you like some?"

"Oh, that's awfully kind, I would," he said.

"Come in, then."

He followed her into the sitting-room. His smile had disappeared, replaced by a tense sort of gravity. She switched on the electric fire, drew back the crimson curtains which had been keeping the room in a reddish twilight, and went into the kitchen to make the tea. She made some toast too and put it with cups and milk and butter on a tray, carrying them back to the sitting-room.

The fire soon began to take the chill off the atmosphere, but the morning was very cold. She could see through the windows that there was a heavy frost on the trees and bushes, which glittered brilliantly under a sky of palest blue. It was the first time that she had really seen what was outside the windows. There was a very small garden in which some rose bushes, with a few roses still in bloom, stood among tall-growing weeds. The garden was enclosed by a high beech hedge that was badly in need of trimming. It was too high for her to see what lay beyond it.

Putting down the tray, she said, "I've got milk, but no

sugar, I'm afraid. I only got here yesterday afternoon, and I haven't had time yet to lay in supplies."

"That's all right, I don't take sugar," the young man answered. "This is very kind of you, but do you mind my asking, is it true you were at the house yesterday and saw this— this woman?"

She poured out two cups of tea. "I was there and I saw *a* woman. She said she was Miss Sharples, but of course she wasn't."

"You see, the police came to see me last night and asked me a lot of questions about where I'd been and so forth, and they told me about this woman and your seeing her, and . . ." He hesitated and gave his oddly charming, toothy smile. "She sounds awfully like Mrs. Neville, my next-door neighbour, and as soon as the police left I went to see her to warn her that they'd probably be coming to see her soon, but she seemed to be out and her car, a small Renault, wasn't there. So this morning I went round again, but she still wasn't there, so I think she must have gone away. And so I thought of coming to see you to check the description the police gave me. Theirs was only second hand, after all. You see, I wondered, was she at all like this?"

He took a wallet out of a pocket in his leather jacket, took a coloured photograph out of the wallet and held it out to Charlotte.

The woman in the photograph was wearing a bikini, not a winter coat, and her fair hair was not rolled up smoothly, but was tumbled loosely about her shoulders. But Charlotte said at once, "Yes, that's the woman."

"You're sure? You couldn't possibly be mistaken?"

She shook her head.

"Oh God!" he said.

There was so much distress on his face that she said, "She may have nothing to do with the murder, you know.

She may have blundered into it, just as I did. Do you know her well?"

He returned the photograph to his wallet and the wallet to his pocket.

"Rather well," he said. "Only the day before yesterday she agreed to marry me."

CHAPTER THREE

He looked so desperate and apprehensive that Charlotte had to take him seriously, although she found it difficult. He was at least five years younger than the woman she had seen at Brickett's Farm, but it was not the actual years that made the statement surprising to Charlotte. What were five years, after all? It was the fact that he had a look of peculiarly guileless immaturity, while the woman had looked as if she had experienced all too much in her lifetime. But perhaps that was what had made them attractive to one another.

"You called her Mrs. Neville," she said. "Is she a widow?"

"Separated," he answered. "She's got an awful husband who still keeps making trouble for her."

"Have you known her long?"

"Ever since she came here. That's about three months now."

"What brought you here? Have you a job in Mattingley?"

"No, it probably sounds absurd, but I'm a writer. I'm writing a novel. I thought it would only take me a few months, but somehow I keep having to rewrite great chunks of it, and so I don't know when I'm going to get to the end. I'm just hoping my funds don't run out before I get there. I went to Saudi Arabia to teach English in a school there for a couple of years, and I was so well paid and saved so much money I thought I could afford to do this one thing I really wanted to do and write this book." He looked self-conscious as he spread butter on the toast that Charlotte had pushed towards him. "It's really just about myself, and I dare say it isn't going to turn out much good, but I feel I've got to get it out of my system before I can really tackle anything else."

"What will you do if your funds do run out before you've finished it?" Charlotte asked.

"I suppose I might go abroad again, or try to get a job in journalism or something," he said. "I haven't thought about it much. Isobel—that's Mrs. Neville—helped me a great deal. She always let me talk all my difficulties over with her. She always said I was too stark and cold. She said I didn't put enough of myself into it. I dare say she was right. She's a very brilliant woman, I think, although she's never made up her mind to develop any special talent. I think her marriage may have been at the bottom of that. She married very young, before she'd had a chance to find out anything about herself, and her husband was the kind who couldn't bear it if his wife had any interest in life but him. She was supposed just to look after him and be a good hostess for him and help his career along. And she really isn't that sort of woman at all. She was terribly wasted."

"What d'you suppose she was doing at Brickett's Farm yesterday evening?" Charlotte asked. "Just paying the rent, like me?"

He gave a slight shake of his head and his eyes met Charlotte's. She discovered that there was an extraordinary quality of candour in his gaze and thought that if he could keep that look when he was telling a lie, he would be a very dangerous young man. However, why should she expect a lie just then?

"I think she went there to tell Frensham that she and I were going to get married," he said. "It's the only thing I can think of. They'd had an affair, you see. Something pretty intense while it lasted. That's why she came to live here, I believe, although it was partly to get away from her husband. But although she and Frensham had never actually broken things off, they really both lost interest in one another some time ago. All the same, I think she'd feel that to be honest with him, she'd got to tell him straight away about our getting married and not leave him to find out from somebody else. That would be like her. She's a wonderfully honest person."

Charlotte was beginning to feel that for Isobel Neville to live up to Ian Havershaw's picture of her might turn out to be as much of a strain as meeting the demands made on her by her first husband. For certainly the woman whom she had met at Brickett's Farm had not been wonderfully honest. Thinking of the readiness with which she had allowed herself to be identified as Miss Sharples and of that quick flick of her glove as she tried to hide the betraying wedding-ring, Charlotte felt sure that she was a naturally devious person who had easily succeeded in giving this young man a totally misleading picture of herself.

Yet even if he was guileless in his fashion, he was not, she thought, a fool.

"Did you know Mr. Frensham well?" she asked.

"Not very. We'd chat a bit when we met by chance, but we'd nothing in common. He was the sort of man who despised anyone who thought differently from himself, and he was a rather violent man, I think. That's just an intuition, actually. I've no evidence of it. But I can't stand violence. The love of it seems to me to be the really fundamental evil in human nature. That's what a good deal of my book's about. Of course, he thought I was insane, trying to write, when I might be earning what he'd call an honest living."

"He didn't do much about earning an honest living himself, did he?" Charlotte poured out second cups of tea for

th. "He seems to have been quite happy a
t of his stepmother's. But I was just wondering
re his affair with Mrs. Neville was over from his po
of view as well as hers? Because, if it wasn't, and if, as yo
say, he was a violent man, isn't there a possibility that he
threatened her and she shot him in self-defence?"

"She hadn't a gun," he said quickly.

"How do you know?"

"I—I just do know. She wasn't that kind of person."

"Had you ever talked about it? For instance, had you
ever talked about whether or not she could shoot?"

"Of course not. Why should we talk about a thing like
that?"

"Well, if your book's mainly about violence and you and
she discussed it a lot, I thought the subject might somehow
have come up."

"My book isn't about that kind of violence." He was
becoming excited. His cheeks had flushed and his lips were
drawn back tightly, showing his uneven teeth. "It's about
the kind of violence you feel inside yourself when all you do
about it is say one unkind word which is never forgotten,
and though nothing more is ever said or done about it, a
relationship goes on the rocks. Nothing shows, yet everything's changed. That's what I'm trying to show. It's mostly
about a mother and son and the awful things they do to one
another although they both believe they love one another
intensely."

Charlotte felt that she had heard this plot before.

"Then of course I was wrong," she said. "But suppose
Mr. Frensham did threaten Mrs. Neville with a gun and she
struggled and got it away from him and it went off by accident and killed him. Do you think that's possible? She was
in a pretty terrible state when I saw her. I realized she was
terrified of something."

⌐ gone to see him and found him murdered.
⌐n't that upset anybody?"

⌐et she hadn't called the police, which surely would
⌐ve been the natural thing to do. And if he was dead al-
⌐eady when she got there, how did she get into the house?
Had she a key?"

"I'm sure she hadn't. When they met, it was always in her
cottage. His stepmother lived in the house, remember, and
Miss Sharples was generally around too."

"So it might have been the murderer himself who let her
in, or who left the door open behind him when he left. In either case, she probably knows who it was, and I suppose
that's why she's vanished. She realizes she's in danger herself."

The excitement had faded from his face, leaving it looking too drained and worn for his age. She had a feeling that
he had been over all this already by himself.

"You may be right," he muttered almost absently, then
stood up without having drunk his second cup of tea. "Anyway, I expect I'll hear from her soon. I expect she'd have
telephoned by now if only there was a phone in the cottage.
But I'll probably get a letter from her tomorrow. Thank you
for talking. When I came I wasn't even sure she was the
woman you'd seen in the house. Now there's no doubt of
it."

He turned to the door and let himself out, but left Charlotte to close it behind him.

She did so, then returned to her breakfast, picking up her
cup, nursing it between both hands and sipping from it as
she brooded on the relationship between Edgar Frensham
and Isobel Neville. It appeared to arouse no jealousy in Ian
Havershaw. He had said only one or two derogatory things
about Edgar Frensham and seemed to have no fear of any
power he might still have exerted over Isobel Neville, far

less any resentment of his mere existence. But was it normal to be as free of jealousy as that? Charlotte herself had never achieved it. On the occasions when she had almost succeeded in falling in love, she had been jealous, suspicious and demanding.

Finishing her tea, she carried the breakfast things out to the kitchen, washed them, then went upstairs to dress.

From her bedroom window she could see over the beech hedge to Brickett's Farm, which stood on a slight rise among tall cedars. Its roof this morning shone with a frosty lustre. The meadow between the cottage and the house was white, except where faint rainbows had formed on the crystaline covering of the grass. After last night's rain the roads would be paved with ice. A good day for staying indoors, she thought. She had a wash, dressed in the same sweater and slacks that she had worn the day before, made her bed and went downstairs again.

The wintry sun, pale as it was, started a thaw about halfway through the morning. She presently became aware of the sound of dripping from the eaves and when she looked out of the window, she saw that the beech hedge had shed most of its silvering of frost. At the same time she heard a sound that she had been half-expecting for some time, footsteps coming crunching up the path from the gate to the door. Detective Superintendent Barr, or some underling, she thought, as she went to the door and opened it.

But it was a woman who stood there, a woman of about forty, of medium height and of a fragile, bony build, with sharp, bird-like features, short black hair and small, shining dark eyes. She was wearing tight black slacks, tucked into black boots and a black, quilted anorak over a high-necked white sweater.

"Good morning," she said. "I'm Angela Bird, a neighbour. I live in the cottage a little way beyond the gates. Tell me if it's a nuisance, my calling in, because of course if it is I'll go. But I thought perhaps, things being as they are, you might prefer not be left all alone."

"That's very kind of you," Charlotte said. "Come in."

The other woman stepped over the threshold. For someone whose name was Bird, Charlotte thought, she looked almost too fantastically like an oyster catcher, so slender, so delicate in her movements, so beady-eyed, and all in black and white.

"Are you all right here?" the woman asked. "Got everything you want? Quite comfortable?"

"Oh yes, thank you," Charlotte answered. "Everything's fine. That's to say, I mean . . ." She left it at that.

Miss Bird gave a little cackle. "Oh, I know what you mean. Except for a murder you could have done without on the very night you arrived. Does that sound callous? Yes, of course it does. But what's the point of being anything else when crocodile tears won't help anybody? If they would, believe me, I'd shed them with the best will in the world. I don't approve of murder. But as everyone knows, Edgar and I detested one another, and as nothing I can do will bring him back to life, why should I put on an act of heavy mourning? But perhaps you find this offensive. You and he may have been great friends."

"I hardly knew him," Charlotte answered. She and Miss Bird had both sat down near the fire. "I'm sorry I can't offer you a drink, but I've nothing in the house."

"Don't give it a thought," Miss Bird said, leaning back and crossing one slim black leg over the other. "As a matter of fact, I came in to ask you if you'd like to come round for drinks this evening. If you think it's bad taste to have a party of sorts, even a very small one, at the moment, just say so, but I thought it would be a good idea for those of us who live round here to get together and tell each other what we know. And also I thought it might be a good thing for you to meet a few of us and not feel too isolated at a time like this. It'll be a very quiet affair, of course, just a gathering of some neighbours. We shan't exactly revel. Still, if you'd sooner not come, I shan't be offended."

"I'd like to come—thank you," Charlotte said.

"Good. About six o'clock. It's the white thatched cottage beyond the gates called Honeysuckle Cottage. You'll find all the cottages on the estate have botanical names. It was a fancy of old Mrs. Frensham's. You haven't met her, I suppose."

"Do you mean Mr. Frensham's stepmother?"

"Yes, that's right. Do you know, she's ninety-four. She was years older than Edgar's father when they married, but I believe she was a great beauty in her time, as well as very rich, so it wasn't too surprising. Anyway, she's always been pretty good to Edgar, though of course she bullied him infamously. If she'd been the one who was murdered, instead of him, I'd have been certain he'd done it. But I shouldn't think you'd be likely to take to murder suddenly at the age of ninety-four, unless perhaps you felt you'd had most other experiences in life, but you still felt something was missing."

"But there's the problem that her chair-lift was out of order," Charlotte said, "or rather, had been turned off downstairs and she was marooned at the top."

"That's interesting. So it was someone who knew the ways of the house. And how would she have got rid of the gun, I wonder? The police told me it's missing, and she couldn't have gone far without help." Miss Bird stood up. Black, white and gaunt, in some curious way impressive, there was something forbidding about her in spite of her friendliness. "But that house was always terribly full of conflict, you know. There was a great deal of hatred and distrust under the surface. Edgar was a very easy person to

hate, if you knew him well, and the old woman's a scream-
ing mass of bitterness and envy. She can't endure having
outlived her beauty and tries to use her money to take its
place. But that kind of hatred sometimes helps to keep people going, doesn't it? They were very dependent on one another. I don't know how she'll manage now without him.
Perhaps she'll just pack up and die. It wouldn't surprise me.
Well, don't forget, six o'clock, unless you change your mind
about coming, or something unexpected happens, in which
case there's no need to let me know. Good-bye."

She stalked to the door and let herself out.

Holding it open after her until she had disappeared
through the gate, Charlotte stood there wondering what
kind of unexpected event Miss Bird anticipated that might
stop her going to the party. The arrest of a murderer or
murderess? The necessity to identify a tall, blonde woman,
alive or dead? Another murder?

In spite of the thaw, the air entering at the open door was
very cold. Charlotte shut it quickly and went back to the
fire.

A visit from the police, about half-past twelve, hardly
qualified as an unexpected event. She had felt sure that they
would come sooner or later. When her door-knocker rattled
again she found Superintendent Barr and a young sergeant
on the doorstep. Mr. Barr had the hollow-eyed look of
someone who has been up for most of the night, but his
smooth, ruddy cheeks were as fresh and shiny as if he had
only just shaved. With his towering presence in the room, it
seemed to shrink. None of the wicker chairs looked large
enough to hold him. Yet he settled quite comfortably into
one of them, while the sergeant took a chair at the table,
brought a note-pad out of his pocket and also a cellophane

envelope that contained another envelope, which he handed
to the Superintendent.

He looked at it musingly, as if he were not quite sure if
he had seen it before, then took a sheet of paper out of it,
unfolded it and, as if it might somehow have changed since
he had seen it last, carefully read it through before holding
it out to Charlotte.

"What do you make of this, Miss Cambrey?" he asked.
"We found it on the blotter on Mr. Frensham's desk." He
showed her the envelope, which had a stamp on it, but had
plainly never been posted. "You see, it's addressed to me,
and we think it must have been on the desk when you and
Mrs. Frensham and Miss Sharples were in the office yesterday evening, but none of you has said anything about seeing
it there. Do you remember it?"

Charlotte hesitated before reaching out for the sheet of
paper.

He went on, "It's all right, take it. It's been tested for
finger-prints, and there were none on it but Mr. Frensham's."

She took the paper, but before reading it made an effort
to envisage what there had been on the desk the evening before. Then she shook her head.

"I can't remember anything about the desk, except that
there were some papers and my rent strewn about on it. All
I remember clearly is sitting there trying not to remember
just how he'd looked in the other room, and the blood on
the carpet there, and feeling sick and wanting to get away
as quickly as possible."

"Quite natural. But will you read that letter now and tell
me how it strikes you?"

She began to read it. At first she did not take in what she
was reading and had to go back to the beginning again and
start it once more. The handwriting, it seemed to her, was

the same as the handwriting of the informal agreement for the lease of the cottage that she had signed the week before, but she could not have said for sure that they were the same.

She read:

"Dear Mr. Barr,

I fear I am burdening you with an unpleasant duty, but at least it will have no personal importance to you, as it might to a closer acquaintance. We have met a few times, but it would not surprise me if you cannot even remember me. If I tell you that I am about to take my own life, you will not feel much distress. Perhaps the people whom I think of as my friends would feel less than I suppose, but I will give them the benefit of the doubt and not put their affection to the test. Not that I shall know anything about it, one way or the other, but it is almost impossible to imagine that total blacking out of knowledge, which I believe will actually follow my act. I am writing to you now merely to insure that no one but myself is blamed for it. I will not go into my reasons for doing it. Enough to say that I have had some shattering news which makes me feel that I simply do not want to go on living. Life, at the best of times, is not such a splendid bargain. I have felt very weary of it for some time. I only regret that there is an unavoidable untidiness about death, which someone other than myself will have to clear up. I am trying to leave as little of this behind as possible, but there is bound to be some unpleasantness. My apologies for asking you to handle this for me and my thanks for whatever you may see fit to do in the circumstances.

Yours sincerely, Edgar Frensham."

Charlotte was frowning by the time that she finished the letter, then held it out to Mr. Barr.

"Read it again," he suggested.

"Isn't that a very odd sort of letter for a suicide to write?" she asked.

"What do you think?"

She read it again.

"No," she said, "it simply isn't what you'd say if you were just going to shoot yourself."

She held the letter out to him once more and he took it, folded it and returned it to its envelope.

"Stamped and addressed quite correctly, as you see," he said as he handed it back to the sergeant. "What do you make of that?"

"It's certainly strange," Charlotte answered. "He must have known Miss Sharples would find him and that the natural thing for her to do would be to telephone the police or Dr. Maynard at once, not post a letter. It's true she was scared of the telephone, but in a crisis like that she'd surely have screwed up her courage to use it, or at least do what she did last night, fetch me or one of the other neighbours."

"Meaning that even if he wanted to leave a letter for me to say he was responsible for his own death, there was no reason for him to put a stamp on it. Miss Sharples could hand it to me. There was no reason for it to go through the post."

She nodded. "Though I suppose at a time like that he mightn't have known quite what he was doing. Putting a stamp on the letter might have been just an automatic action."

"But you feel yourself the letter doesn't read as if it had been written by someone in that sort of state of mind."

"No, it's ever so much too carefully composed. That's

why it doesn't sound real. Is there any possibility that it's a forgery?"

"We haven't been able to go into that thoroughly yet, but our expert in Mattingley thinks it's in Mr. Frensham's writing."

"Then what do you make of it?"

He did not answer. His flat, unblinking stare remained on her face as if he were waiting for her to go on without any prompting from him.

"He didn't commit suicide, did he?" she asked. "He was murdered. Dr. Maynard said if he'd shot himself, he'd have done it sitting down, not standing in the middle of the room."

"Probable, but not certain. Suicides do the strangest things."

"But did you find the gun there?"

"No."

"Then doesn't that mean for sure it was murder?"

"Again, it's probable but not certain. According to your own evidence, at least four people were in the house after Mr. Frensham died—the blonde woman whom we believe to be Mrs. Neville of Jasmine Cottage, old Mrs. Frensham, Miss Sharples and yourself. Any one of you could have removed the gun. It's even possible Dr. Maynard removed it. As I understand it, he was alone in the room with the corpse for some minutes before the police arrived."

"But why should anyone remove the gun? Why try to make suicide look like murder? Is there insurance involved?"

"Not to our knowledge."

"Well, if you think I took the gun, you're at liberty to search Beech Cottage," Charlotte said rather stiffly. Then, as he did not reply, she added, "Actually, you're sure it's murder, aren't you?"

"I'm not sure of anything yet," he said. "There's still that letter to be explained."

"He might have been forced to write it somehow, mightn't he? It could have been dictated. That would explain why it sounds so artificial."

"How can you force a man to write a letter like that?"

"Perhaps he was threatened with torture of some kind if he didn't write it, but promised a nice easy death if he did."

"In that case, we're brought back to asking why the murderer, after going to all that trouble, took the gun away."

She pinched her lower lip between finger and thumb, looking at his stolid face speculatively.

"I think if anyone took the gun away after the suicide had been faked, it must have been Mrs. Neville," she said. "I'm sure now she knew he was dead when I came to the house. Something I remember—I told her I wanted to ask her some questions and she looked absolutely panic-stricken, then when she found I only wanted to know about local shops and things like that, she was so relieved she got quite friendly for a few minutes. Do you know anything about where she's gone?"

"Not at present, but we'll find her sooner or later. She may have had a motive for the murder, the old-fashioned one of jealousy. She was Frensham's mistress for some time —all the people round here seem to have known that—but at the same time he seems to have been having an affair with another woman. We got his safe open this morning and there's a collection of letters in it with dates that show he was carrying on with the two women at the same time. There are no envelopes and no addresses, so we don't know where they were posted, but they're pretty explosive stuff. Threatening too. She seems to have had some knowledge about him that she was threatening to make public if he threw her over. Some of the other documents in the safe are

—well, interesting too. Not that there are many of them. The thing's half empty. However, that isn't what we came to talk about. I wanted to ask you if you've any objection to giving me a specimen of your handwriting."

"To see if I wrote those passionate letters?"

He answered with a steely little smile. "You can refuse, if you want to."

"Oh, I don't mind."

The sergeant handed her his note-pad and his ballpoint pen. She put the pad on her knee.

"What shall I write?"

"Anything you like."

Her mind went blank, then after a moment she wrote quickly, "Accident, suicide, murder—give me murder."

"Sign it, will you?" Mr. Barr said.

She added the words, "Charlotte Cambrey." Her writing was small, neat, slightly sloping and very legible.

The sergeant produced another cellophane envelope from his pocket and handed it to Mr. Barr, who extracted the sheet of paper inside it and laid it down beside the sheet on which Charlotte had written.

"Not the slightest resemblance," he said.

"Is that one of this woman's letters?" she asked.

He nodded, turning the letter so that she had a glimpse of it, but not giving her time to read it. The writing was much larger than Charlotte's, upright, forceful, rather spiky.

"How is it signed?" she asked.

"Just with the letter B." Handing it back to the sergeant, he added, "Of course, you'll understand the point of my inquiry."

"Oh yes," she said. "I realize I'm bound to be on your list of suspects. But do you know that Mrs. Neville got engaged to marry Mr. Havershaw only a few days ago, so she'd no reason to be jealous of this woman any longer, had she?"

The two men stood up.

"Not on the face of it," Mr. Barr said. "But we've only Mr. Havershaw's word for it that they got engaged, just as we've only yours that you ever saw her at Brickett's Farm. You've neither of you any witnesses to what you've told us. Well, thank you for your help, Miss Cambrey. I hope we shan't have to trouble you again too soon."

They left, their footsteps crunching on the icy footpath.

Charlotte suddenly found that she had a strange inclination to tremble and wished again that it had occurred to her to pack a bottle of whisky in her suitcase. For if they did not believe that she had seen the blonde woman the evening before, what did they really think about her? Did they know already why she had really come here? How did they fit her into the chain of events?

She thought of walking into the village to see if there was a pub where she could have a quiet lunch and a drink. But she could imagine only too easily how she would be stared at. She was the girl who had seen and talked with the murderess—wasn't that the story that had probably already gone the round of the neighbourhood? That Mrs. Neville had done the murder was probably considered hardly open to doubt, and Charlotte had almost caught her in the act. She thought that was the real reason why she had been invited to drinks by Miss Bird. She and her friends wanted the full story of what had happened the evening before. When Charlotte arrived at Honeysuckle Cottage, she would be subjected to polite but persistent questioning.

She changed before she set out at six o'clock. She had brought only one dress with her, a red-and-black tweed, which she thought would be more appropriate than her slacks, but her heart sank when her hostess opened the door to her. She was in a long velvet dress, printed with a paisley pattern in peacock colours. Did she deliberately model herself on some bird, Charlotte wondered. This morning it had been an oyster-catcher, now it was a peacock. She looked very handsome in her gaunt, long-legged way.

"Now come and meet everybody," she said, "though I think you've met one or two of them already. Dr. Maynard says he met you yesterday evening, and Ian called in on you this morning, didn't he? But you haven't met Mr. and Mrs. Grainger yet. They live in Rose Cottage, next to me. Now what will you have to drink, sherry, whisky, vodka, gin?"

Charlotte said that she would like sherry. The Graingers had both risen to their feet and were smiling at her diffidently over the glasses that they were holding. They were both about thirty-five, small, neat, brown-haired, mouse-like people. They were the kind of couple who look remarkably like one another, having chosen each other, perhaps, because each was a satisfying mirror-image of the other, which might be a kind of comfort in a world that had never taken much notice of either of them. Mr. Grainger wore a high-necked black jersey, a green tweed jacket and grey slacks. Mrs. Grainger wore a pale blue trouser suit, several strings of beads and large, round ear-rings, made of painted pottery.

They both said that they were pleased to meet Charlotte, said that they hoped she liked her cottage as much as they liked theirs, then they lapsed into silence, looking at her expectantly, as if they thought that with this much encouragement she would have something startling to tell them.

Waiting for her drink, she took in the room with its good modern furniture, its comfortable chairs covered in gay, flowered material, its ornaments—mostly Staffordshire dogs in all shapes and sizes—and its rather indifferent watercolours ranged around the walls. It was certainly not a room that had been furnished by Edgar Frensham for a tenant, but probably by Miss Bird herself. Hadn't someone told Charlotte that Miss Bird had lived here for two years? Yes, Miss Sharples had said it. So naturally it would have been worth her while to move in her own furniture. But what had kept her in this quiet place for so long?

That question was answered during the casual talk with which the party began. Miss Bird, Charlotte learned, was an almoner at the Mattingley Infirmary, but liked to live in the country. She painted a little in her spare time. The watercolours on the walls were her work. Charlotte managed to say something polite about them, at which Miss Bird looked ironic instead of pleased, as if she were aware of how little merit they had. The presence of the Graingers was also explained. They were negotiating for a shop in Mattingley, where they intended to sell what they called novelties, which meant, apparently, china, glass, jewellery, Christmas cards, paperbacks and children's toys. When the deal was concluded they meant to move into Mattingley to live in a flat over the shop, but in the meantime Rose Cottage suited them admirably. Miss Bird told Charlotte that Ian Havershaw was a writer, but he interrupted to say that he had already told her that.

"Have the police been to see you today?" he asked her. "I think they've been round the rest of us. It seems Frensham left a rather curious suicide's letter behind him, yet his death almost certainly wasn't suicide."

"Yes, and they wanted a specimen of my handwriting," Charlotte said. "It seems there are some very passionate letters to Mr. Frensham in his safe, just signed with the letter B, by someone they haven't identified, and they're wondering if that gave Mrs. Neville the motive of jealousy. I told them about your engagement to her, which seemed to me to dispose of that. I hope you don't mind."

"I told them that myself," he answered. "Did you see any of the letters?"

"I had a glimpse of one. The writing was nothing like Mrs. Neville's."

"When have you seen hers?" he asked, puzzled.

"She wrote a receipt for the rent I left for Mr. Frensham. The police have got it now. She signed it E. Sharples, but it was hers. I saw her write it. She told me she was Miss Sharples when I met her, you know."

He nodded glumly. "I got that from the police. But they didn't want a specimen of my writing. They seem to have stuck to the women. Angela, the police asked you for a specimen of your handwriting today, didn't they?"

"Oh yes," Miss Bird answered.

"And mine too," Mrs. Grainger said. "And I've such a terrible writing, I was ashamed to give them one, and I simply couldn't think what to write. In the end I wrote, 'Little Bo-peep has lost her sheep.' Then I had to sign it with my name. I felt so stupid. Angela, of course, writes beautifully. I just love your writing, Angela. I think it comes of your being an artist. You're such a perfectionist. What did you write?"

"'I had not known death had undone so many,'" Miss Bird answered.

"Oh, T. S. Eliot," Ian Havershaw said.

"Dante, actually," Miss Bird corrected him with a slightly condescending smile.

"But what did they say about handwriting?" Dr. Maynard asked.

"Nothing of interest."

"Did they show you one of the letters from the safe?"

"No, they just told me about them."

"But they told you about the letter Edgar left behind him, didn't they, and the gun that seems to be missing?

That's the thing I really don't understand. Suppose that letter was a forgery, or Edgar was somehow forced to write it, why wasn't the gun left behind to back it up?"

"There could be a simple answer to that," Angela Bird said, "though you won't like it. It's just that someone needed the gun rather badly. It's possible, isn't it, that we haven't seen our last murder?"

CHAPTER FOUR

The party broke up about eight o'clock. Dr. Maynard, whose Jaguar was in the road, insisted on seeing Charlotte back the short distance to her cottage, and when they reached it, stood at the gate so stolidly that she felt there was nothing for it but to ask him in.

He accepted the invitation promptly and when she said that she was sorry that she could not offer him another drink, replied that he had already had quite enough for the evening, but would be grateful for a few minutes talk with her. She unlocked the front door, switched on the light and the fire and took his coat from him.

"The fact is," he said, taking up a stand in front of the fire where it comfortably warmed the back of his legs, "I want to ask you a few rather personal questions. If you don't want to answer them, just say so at once. I realize I've no special right to ask them."

"Go ahead," she said as she sat down in one of the wicker chairs.

"You see, I've known the Frenshams for a number of years," he said. "I probably know them more intimately than any of the other people around here, because Mrs. Frensham's needed a good deal of attendance. But I've never heard them mention you. May I ask how long you've known them?"

"I saw Mrs. Frensham for the first time in my life yesterday evening," Charlotte answered. "I spoke to Mr. Frensham for the first time on the telephone last week, and I arranged then to come down last Saturday and see the cottage, which I thought would just suit me. It isn't surprising they've never mentioned me."

"How did you hear the cottage was vacant?"

"I saw it advertised in a Sunday paper."

"You didn't hear about it from anyone here?"

"No, I've never met any of them before today."

"And you haven't met a Miss Beatrice Wallace either?" She shook her head. "I've never heard of her."

He looked at her curiously. His round, comfortable face had its detached, professional look, as if he were trying to pry out of her a description of symptoms which, out of fear, she was trying to conceal from him.

"She was a nurse here for some time after Mrs. Frensham had her stroke," he said. "As a matter of fact, I recommended her. She was a very competent woman. Later I wondered if she was just the most satisfactory sort of person . . ." He hesitated. "You said those letters in the safe were signed with the letter B."

"So Mr. Barr told me."

"Surprising," he said. "I don't mean on her side. Edgar Frensham was very attractive to a certain kind of woman. But she wasn't a very attractive sort of woman herself. Plain, a bit domineering, brusque. Perfectly splendid in a crisis, but not tactful or gentle. That's why I thought I'd made a mistake, sending her to look after Mrs. Frensham, who's a somewhat domineering woman herself. Someone quieter and less opinionated would probably have been able to handle her far better than Nurse Wallace."

"You feel sure she wrote those letters?" Charlotte asked.

"Well, as I said, it surprises me, but that sort of hard, cold exterior can easily hide a mass of emotion. And she and Frensham were exposed to each other every day. So it does seem probable, doesn't it? And I asked you if you'd met her because she stayed in this cottage for a time after she'd left Brickett's Farm. There was some sort of row between her and Miss Sharples, who's an excellent woman, but very possessive where Mrs. Frensham's concerned, and Frensham offered Nurse Wallace this cottage while she looked for other work. She wasn't actually needed at Brickett's any more. Miss Sharples was quite capable of looking after Mrs. Frensham, who'd made a fairly good recovery, considering her age. Then Miss Wallace kept the cottage on for quite a while as a sort of home for herself while she went out to other jobs. Incidentally, it was she who advised putting that chair-lift in for Mrs. Frensham, which has turned out an excellent idea."

"Where is she now?"

"I'm not sure, but I rather think she's gone to Madeira with an elderly couple who can't stand the winter in this climate." He gave his buttocks a little pat, as if to make sure that they had been sufficiently warmed, then moved away from the fire. "Did the police mention anything else they found in the safe besides those letters?"

"They said there wasn't much else in it, but that what there was was 'interesting.' That was their word for it."

"What do you suppose they meant by it?"

"I don't know, but I'd a feeling they meant something— well, a bit dubious. Something Mr. Frensham wanted kept secret rather than anything valuable."

"I see. Yes. Well, I mustn't keep you." He picked up his coat again. "I always wondered about that safe, you know, what he had that needed locking away so carefully. But that's all that the police told you about it, is it? That there were those letters from a woman called B and some other 'interesting' items?"

"Yes, that's all."

" 'Interesting' is a word that's sometimes used to cover pornography. But that doesn't sound like Frensham. He wasn't a man who troubled to conceal his vices. Well, good-night, Miss Cambrey. We'll meet again soon, I'm sure. By the way, how long are you intending to stay?"

"I took the cottage for a month, but I'm not sure if I shall stay as long as that, unless the police insist on it. I haven't been very well and I came here for a rest, but the atmosphere isn't exactly restful."

"I'm so sorry. You look the picture of health, you know. But of course, looks can be deceptive."

He gave her another of his kindly, assessing glances, then said good-night once more and left.

Charlotte went to the kitchen, made herself some scrambled eggs and tea, took them to the living-room, sat down by the fire, picked up her book and ate and read slowly.

The quiet of the room was pleasant after the battering she had had all day from the human voice. By degrees she relaxed, closed her eyes and in a little while drifted off to sleep.

When she woke presently, she took her supper things out to the kitchen and went upstairs to bed. But now she slept fitfully, haunted by dreams of anxiety and frustration, and woke at about eight o'clock, glad to be fully awake at last yet feeling tired and obscurely frightened. She was not aware of any cause for her fear, yet it stayed with her, a faint menacing shadow, while she dressed, then went downstairs to make her breakfast. The fear faded only as she began to forget her dreams.

Presently, she thought, she would go into the village and see what she could buy there in the way of food. She would also see if she could buy a newspaper. It would be interesting to see if Edgar Frensham had made his way onto the front page, or onto any page at all, murder being the commonplace event that it is nowadays. For the television that she had thought of hiring she would probably have to go into Mattingley. But did she want one, after all? If she was not going to stay here for more than another few days, which was what she thought probable at the moment, she could get on well enough without one.

She was just leaving the cottage, wearing her sheepskin jacket over her sweater and slacks and carrying a shopping-basket, when a young man came in at the gate. He was in his early twenties, small, dressed in a duffle coat and jeans, with unkempt brown hair almost to his shoulders. It turned out that the was a representative of a local newspaper and that while his colleagues from London were pursuing their inquiries at Brickett's Farm and with the police in Mat-tingley, it had occurred to him to seek out a few of the local people and ask them what they knew about Edgar Frensham.

He had picked up the information, apparently from Miss Sharples, that Charlotte had been in the house before Miss Sharples herself had discovered the body and had met a mysterious blonde woman there. Charlotte did not try to deny this, but that the blonde woman had almost certainly been Isobel Neville and that the only mysteries about her were what she had been doing in the house, calling herself Miss Sharples, and what had happened to her since she had left it, were things that Charlotte thought it wiser not to mention. For all she knew, Mrs. Neville was back in her cottage by now, with a perfectly adequate explanation of all her actions. Charlotte did not invite the young man into the cottage, but chatted to him for a little while at the gate, then set off towards the village to do her shopping.

The ice had melted and the road was muddy. In the day-light she had a better view than she had had the evening be-fore of Miss Bird's cottage. It was white and thatched, de-murely picturesque, with its front door and window-frames painted a delicate yellow, and a great tangle of honeysuckle, which had given it its name, hung over its porch.

A little way beyond it was another cottage, built probably between the wars, a flimsy-looking structure covered with cream-coloured rough-cast, with its woodwork painted a jam-like dark red. The name, "Rose Cottage" was neatly lettered on its gate, and its front was covered with unpruned, climbing roses. This must be where the Graingers lived, Charlotte thought, and supposed that the state of the roses and the quantity of weeds in the small flowerbeds was due to the fact that they were only temporary tenants. Miss Bird's garden, by contrast, showed loving care.

It did not take Charlotte more than five minutes to reach the first houses of the village. The first building was a garage with petrol pumps beside the road, then came a row of council houses, then a pub, then a triangular village green, surrounded by houses of the kind that nowadays are mostly inhabited by retired civil servants, academics, army people and an artist or two, and beyond the green there was a post-office, a grocer's shop and a butcher's. The grocer's was a wonderfully neat little self-service shop that sold nearly everything, including newspapers, some ironmongery, vegetables, a surprising variety of drinks and frozen foods. Charlotte bought the bottle of whisky that she had wished that she had had the day before, a frozen pizza for her lunch, coffee, fresh bread, a number of odds and ends and, planning to make a stew that would last her for several days, some onions and carrots. Then she went on to the butcher's and bought a pound of stewing steak. She almost forgot the newspaper and had to go back to the grocer's for it.

As if she knew why Charlotte wanted it, the woman behind the cash desk said, "Nothing interesting about our troubles here yet. They're too busy with people on strike everywhere and a hurricane somewhere or other and hijacking and all that—nasty stuff, I don't like to read about it. All sensationalism, that's what it is."

Agreeing that it was, Charlotte paid for the newspaper and left.

When she arrived back at Beech Cottage she found that she had another visitor. He was sitting on the bench in the small porch that projected above her front door. When she opened the gate, she could see only his legs, but as soon as he heard the squeak of the gate he got to his feet and she recognized the sandy-haired man who had sat opposite to her in the train from Paddington. He seemed to have been waiting for her for some time. His thin, unmemorable features looked pinched with the cold.

"Good morning," he said. "Not too bad, is it? In fact, not bad at all for the time of year, though not really the weather for sitting out of doors. I hoped you wouldn't be gone too long."

"Don't you ever talk about anything but the weather?" she asked.

"Well, I do, of course," he said, "but I think it often helps with opening up a conversation. Shows one's good intentions, like some of those tribal dances in Africa, which show you come as friends, not enemies. And face it, in this country we're all genuinely interested in the weather. All of us. It's the one thing that binds us together."

"Why do you want to open a conversation with me at all?" Charlotte asked.

She did not unlock the door, but stood still on the path.

"Well, I thought I recognized you in the train the other day," he said, "and now I'm sure of it, after what's happened. I'd particularly like a few words with you, as you will understand."

"Are you a journalist?" she asked.

"No."

"Then who are you?"

"My name's Timothy Royle," he answered.

"That doesn't mean anything to me."

He put a hand into a pocket, brought out a wallet, extracted a card from it and held it out to her.

She read, "Hargreave's Private Inquiry Agency. For immediate and personal investigations. 37 Joad Street, London W.C.1."

"A detective," she said.

She gave him back his card.

"That's right," he said, "and in deeper water than I expected."

"You weren't expecting murder?"

"Hardly."

"Who hired you?"

"You can't expect me to tell you that."

"Was it Edgar Frensham?"

"I'm sorry—no comment."

"Then why should I talk to you, if you won't tell me anything?"

He wriggled his thin shoulders. "If we could go indoors, perhaps, where we could talk comfortably, I could tell you a few things. How I recognized you in the train, for instance."

"The odd thing is, I felt sure I'd seen you somewhere before," she said. "It was at the trial, I suppose." She took her key out of her handbag and unlocked the door. "And that's why you were so interested in why I was coming to Mattingley."

Following her inside, he said, "I'm more interested now in why you're staying. Frensham dead can't help you. Won't the police let you go?"

She put her shopping-basket down on the table, switched on the fire and took off her jacket.

"I haven't asked them," she said. "I've got an idea that if I stay I may find out something useful, even if I can't get anything out of Frensham himself. It's rather a forlorn hope, I know, but since I'm here, I may as well stay at least a few days. Would you like a drink?"

"There's nothing I'd like better. I'm frozen to the marrow." He took off his coat and folded it over a chair.

She took the bottle of whisky out of the basket, took it out to the kitchen, poured out two drinks and brought them back to the living-room. They both sat down and, sipping their drinks, eyed one another with a wary kind of curiosity.

After a moment Charlotte said, "Well, how's the family?"

"Family?" he said.

"Those five children."

"Oh, them, yes. Oh, they're fine. I had a nice talk with the youngest on the telephone last night. She loves the telephone."

"What are their names?"

"Deborah, Vanessa, Theresa, Sandra and Judy."

"All girls. So I suppose you'll keep on and on till you get a boy, and his sisters will all adore him and be furiously jealous of him and bully him and spoil him and he simply won't stand a chance in life."

"As a matter of fact," he said, "we think we've enough now, though of course it would have been nice if one of them had been a boy. But my wife says she's tired of the whole business, so we'd better stop. Which reminds me, I must be thinking of Christmas presents for them. A terrible job that, getting the right thing for the right child, so that you don't get howls of envy instead of thanks. But that isn't what you want me to tell you, is it? I know you said you didn't see why you should tell me anything if I didn't tell you anything about myself, but you can't be much interested in the kids."

"Well then, go on and tell me some other things."

"There isn't much to tell really," he said. "I wasn't involved in your brother's case. I was at his trial because I was interested in the one coming after it. But I saw you there, listening with a kind of incredulous horror to the whole thing, and I saw what an appalling shock it was when he was convicted. Your face just then wasn't the kind of thing it's easy to forget. And when Frensham was giving his evidence you looked at him with a kind of hatred that would have scared me if I'd been him. I can't remember anyone ever looking at me like that."

"Aren't you being wise after the event?" she said. "He's been murdered, so you're remembering how murderous I looked that day. Do you think I did it?"

He gave his head a dubious shake. "I think, if that's what you'd come for, you'd have covered your tracks more carefully. You wouldn't have taken this cottage in your own name. You wouldn't have hung around after the murder. And as I said just now, Frensham dead can't help you. As a matter of fact, I don't think he'd have been much help to you alive either, but that's why you came, isn't it? To see if somehow you could get him to change his evidence."

She gave a tired sigh, leaning back in her chair and watching the whisky in her glass swirl as she twisted it this way and that.

"It was a stupid idea, wasn't it?" she said. "Childish, probably. But I felt I had to try to do something. Do you think my brother's guilty?"

"I've no feelings about it, one way or the other."

"But didn't you look at him in the dock and say to yourself that a boy like that, a quiet, good-mannered, well-educated boy like that, simply couldn't have been capable of a crime like bank robbery?"

"Oh, my dear," he said, with more feeling in his voice than she had heard in it before, "if you'd seen what I have! The case I'd gone to the Old Bailey to listen to that day was one of rape and murder. A girl of seventeen had been given a lift home from a dance by a man she knew quite well, and he raped her and strangled her and threw her body into a ditch, then went home to his wife and kids. And looking at him you'd have thought he was the kind of schoolteacher all the children love, or a bank clerk who'd never touch a penny of your money. You can't tell anything by just looking at people."

"But if you'd known Dick . . . no." She sighed again. "You didn't, so it's a silly thing to say. It's different for me. I simply knew he couldn't have committed the crime. And since I knew that, it meant to me there was something wrong with the evidence against him. And the main evidence was given by Edgar Frensham. You remember, he said he'd gone into that bank in the Strand with his banker's card to cash a cheque, and he was waiting for his turn when three men came in with guns, held the place up, got the money and got away. At least, two of them got away. Frensham said that as they were leaving he rushed the last of them and got his gun away from him and knocked him out, and it was Dick. But of course it wasn't like that. He came in just after the men with the guns and tried to turn and dash out and give an alarm when Frensham stopped him. In the scuffle nobody really saw what happened and nobody could get out, and by the time they did the men and the van they'd come in had gone."

"But what about the girl who handed the money over?" Timothy Royle asked. "Didn't she identify your brother?"

"Not at first. To begin with she was too shocked to remember anything. And it was the same with one or two other people in the bank. They said at first they couldn't swear to anything, then when Frensham was so positive and when they found Dick holding the gun they'd planted on him, they began to have second thoughts and become positive too. And now Dick's doing five years for a crime he didn't commit. It's wicked and it's horrible, and I felt I had to do something about it. Then just by chance I saw the advertisement that this cottage was to let and I thought I'd come here and at least try to get to know Edgar Frensham. I thought he was probably just a busybody who was honestly mistaken, but I didn't think it could do any harm to try to find out a little more about him. But I was too late. All the same, for the moment I'm staying on to see if something comes out about him that might help. If the police dig up the fact that there was something dubious, for instance, they might be ready to reconsider the evidence he gave at the trial."

"It's pretty difficult to get a re-trial once a person's been convicted, you know," Timothy Royle said, emptying his glass and looking at it hopefully, as if he thought that by concentrating on it, he might make it fill itself again. "I can tell you one thing, however, and that is that Frensham was definitely a crook and the police know it. But they also happen to have dug up the fact that you're Dick Cambrey's sister and they're very interested in what you're doing here."

"I suppose that was inevitable," she said. "Perhaps I should have told them about it myself."

"It might have been advisable."

She leant forward and took his empty glass. "You'd like another?"

"That would be very nice."

She went out to the kitchen and refilled his glass.

Returning, she asked, "How do you know so much about what the police think?"

"I've been talking to one or two of them, picking up things here and there."

She looked at him doubtfully. "What do you mean about them knowing that Frensham was a crook?"

"They'd only to get the safe open to be quite sure of it."

"They've told you what they found?"

"Not the police, actually. But I understand there were some letters there from a woman I believe they told you about, love letters, some of them threatening to expose something or other. But apart from that there are some documents and photographs which Frensham was almost certainly using to black-mail certain people."

"I've asked you already, was Frensham your client?"

He raised his eyebrows. They were fine-drawn and a little puckish. The whisky and the warmth of the fire had brought a little colour into his cheeks and his sudden smile had a friendly kind of mockery in it.

"I wonder why you think that," he said.

"Only that a black-mailer might have a use for the services of a private detective. You might be able to root out information for him that he could use."

"If I was ready to do that, why shouldn't I go a step further and do the black-mailing myself?"

"I don't know. Perhaps that's what you do."

His smile broadened. "That's the sort of idea people like you always have about people like me. In fact, if I went in for that kind of thing, I shouldn't last long in my job."

"Then Frensham wasn't your client?"

"Well, if you like, I'll admit he wasn't. But I'm not saying any more than that till I've been given permission to do so."

"I suppose the fact is you were hired by one of the people against whom there's incriminating evidence of some sort in that safe. How were you to get it, by threatening Frensham somehow, or by breaking and entering and opening the safe?"

"Didn't I tell you I wasn't saying any more about all that? But I'll tell you something that may not have occurred to you. The threatening letters from that woman and these other papers, they're all there in the safe still, aren't they? And doesn't that mean that none of the people concerned committed the murder? Because they'd have known the evidence Frensham had against them was still in the safe and they'd have known a murder would bring to light just what they wanted to hide. So I believe that either the murder had nothing to do with anything that was ever in the safe, or else that the murderer managed to make Frensham open it and give him whatever he wanted before he murdered him."

"Is that what the police think too?"

"Well, I put the point to Barr, but I'm not sure if I convinced him. He may be thinking quite correctly that people sometimes act irrationally. They may kill out of hate or fear, without much thought for the consequences."

"Or suppose they think the murderer killed Frensham and thought he had the rest of the evening to open the safe to get what he wanted out of it. So he switched off the lift, so that Mrs. Frensham couldn't interrupt him, and got to work. Then Mrs. Neville came in and he had to make up his mind in a hurry whether to kill her too or do a bolt. And for some reason he chose not to kill her."

"You don't think Mrs. Neville herself was the murderess?"

"Do you?"

"Oh, I haven't got around to thinking anything special yet."

"But you've heard about her?"

He nodded. The slight movement of his head made Charlotte aware of how still he had been sitting, how steadily and attentively he had been watching her. His face, she thought, was more intelligent than she had recognized at first. It was not really a commonplace face except when he felt inclined to make it so. Perhaps he had forgotten to do that during the last few minutes, or thought that he might get farther with her if he dropped the mask.

"Is that really what you came to see me about, to ask me about her?" she asked.

He stretched out his thin legs in front of him, crossing his ankles, while he nursed his glass in both hands.

"Partly, of course," he said, "but also to check up on why you came here, and you've told me that already. I don't think it was a good idea you had, and it might have been dangerous if Frensham had realized what you'd come for. In a way it puzzles me that apparently he didn't. Cambrey isn't the commonest of names. You'd think he must have connected you with your brother. However, even though Frensham himself is dead, it could still be dangerous. Have you thought of that?"

"No," she said, surprised. "Why should it be?"

"Only that if he was involved in that bank robbery, he'd accomplices, hadn't he? Or he was an accomplice, and somewhere there's the man who organized it. And if it turns out that you're trying to stir things up, you might end up as he did. And that would be a pity."

"You think he was killed by someone involved in that crime?"

"Not necessarily, but it's a point to bear in mind. And about the blonde woman . . ."

"Yes?"

"You realize Barr isn't convinced you saw her at all? He isn't sure you saw anyone."

"But I did!"

"I didn't say I don't believe you. But Barr's in two minds

about it. Knowing your connection with your brother, he's ready to wonder a good deal about it. You're far the best suspect he's turned up yet. You see that, don't you?"

"But I've told you," she said, suddenly drumming on her knees with her fists, "Dick's never done anything wrong. There's no reason to suspect me of anything because of him."

"Had he really never been in trouble before?"

"Oh, he got into trouble once going joy-riding with a friend in a neighbour's car. The car was recovered, and he admitted what he'd done and was bound over. It wasn't serious."

"How long ago was that?"

"Look," she said, "I don't know why I'm telling you all this. I don't even know for certain that you're who you say you are."

"I'd say you've been talking because you've been wanting to talk for a long time," he said. "Keeping it bottled up inside you hasn't done you any good. You're not absolutely certain, are you, that your brother had nothing to do with the crime?"

She leant back in her chair, letting her hands flop loosely on either side of her. It puzzled her, now that she came to think of it, why she had told this man as much as she had. He had had no way of compelling her to do so. She had talked willingly, glad in a way, as he had said, to tell her story to someone. Yet he did not fit in any way with her picture of the ideal confidant. It was true that she had begun to think him a more perceptive kind of man than she had at first, and she realized that there was a good deal of intelligence hidden away behind that carefully nondescript face. But there had not been much sympathy there. There had been no sign, as he questioned her, that he wanted to help her.

As if he were put out by her continuing distrust of him, he said in a gentler tone than before, "Your brother didn't live with you, did he?"

She gave herself a moment to decide whether or not she would answer any more of his questions, but she could see no harm in this one.

"He did for a time, but more recently he'd been living with a girl in a flat in Clapham. He hadn't had a job for some time. He was never very good at keeping jobs. There was always something better he might get if he went after it. The girl was a librarian, and almost as soon as Dick went to prison she got married to a man who also worked in the library. Dick didn't seem surprised about it when I told him. I think he'd been expecting it."

"But you don't think that that could have had anything to do with the crime," he said. "I mean, if he thought he was losing her and was desperate and thought that if only he had money she'd stick to him, mightn't he have done something that seems to you quite unlike himself?"

"He wasn't desperate, he didn't mind losing her all that much, and he didn't commit the crime."

He gave her one of his ironic grins. "You're very loyal. Well, that's nice. I like it. I assume you haven't any parents, or you wouldn't feel so responsible for him."

"My father died when I was a child," she said. "I hardly remember him. My mother died three years ago of cancer. Until she died my brother and I lived with her, then he stayed with me for a time, as I told you, till he joined his girl friend in Clapham."

He stood up. "Well, as I said, I like loyalty. And this talk's confidential, if that's what you want it to be."

"I don't think I care much," she said. "I'll probably tell it all to the police sooner or later anyhow."

"Good-bye, then. Thanks for the whisky."

When he had gone she sat for a time trying to remember what she had actually told him, wondering if there was anything important that she wished she had not said. All of it, she decided in the end. She had let herself drift into a half-intimate mood with him, though he had told her almost nothing about himself. He had said that he was a private detective, but had she any proof of it? His card could have been forged or stolen. He had refused to tell her who had employed him. His presence here had certainly something to do with Edgar Frensham, but who was there in Frensham's circle who was likely to hire a private detective? Frensham himself, or someone who had been a victim of his black mail. If it was true that Frensham had been a black-mailer. The police had not told her so. She had only Timothy Royle's word for it. And some intuition told her not to believe quite everything he said. A devious character, she thought. Not someone to talk to freely.

The door-knocker rattled again.

She went to the door and opened it. It was Timothy Royle back again.

"There's someone in Mrs. Neville's cottage," he said. "There's a car in the garage and I saw someone at a window. A woman, I think. D'you feel inclined to come along and see if you recognize her?"

CHAPTER FIVE

It was not a woman who opened the door of Jasmine Cottage to Charlotte and Timothy Royle. It was a man of about thirty-five, dressed in a high-necked white sweater and dark red velvet trousers. But it was easy to see why Royle, having only a glimpse of him through a window, had taken him for a woman. His thick, auburn hair, which fell in soft waves round his face, was carefully cut and shaped. He was very slender, with narrow shoulders and smooth, delicately moulded features. His greenish eyes had long, curling lashes. Not that Royle could have noticed such things as eyelashes through a window, but the man's whole appearance had a touch of the feminine about it.

But there was nothing feminine about his voice when he said, "Now what do *you* want?" It was a deep resonant voice with a growl of intense impatience in it.

The cottage was further from the village than the others and even in daylight would have been invisible from them. It was at the end of a drive that turned sharply off the main road, passing what looked like a barn, except that it had curtains at the windows, as if somebody lived there too. Jasmine Cottage looked older than the others, with black beams supporting bulging walls, small, casement windows and a roof of moss-grown tiles. But indoors it looked much the same as Charlotte's cottage. The front door opened straight into a small living-room in which there were wicker chairs and a plastic and metal table. As in her room, there was a vase on the table. It had a few sprays of cotoneaster in it, but the leaves were withered and most of the scarlet berries had dropped and were scattered around the vase. Also a writing-table in a corner of the room, just like hers, had all its drawers open, with papers spilled out of them on to the floor. The man, whoever he was, seemed to have been making a hurried search through them when Charlotte and Royle had interrupted him.

"I'm sorry," Royle said. "We were looking for Mrs. Neville. I saw someone in here and thought she might have got back."

"Who are you?" the man asked harshly.

"This is Miss Cambrey," Royle said, "and my name's Timothy Royle. We're neighbours. Do you mind telling us who you are?"

"I don't see what business it is of yours," the man answered, "but I'm Marcus Neville. Isobel's husband. Do you know where she is?"

"No, she vanished on Saturday night in slightly mysterious circumstances. If she'd come back, we wanted to make sure she was all right." Royle spoke quietly and smoothly, just as if what he was saying was the truth.

"You'd better come in," the man said. "I don't know what you mean by mysterious circumstances. You'd better explain."

He held the door open and Charlotte and Royle went down the two steep steps into the room. Marcus Neville closed the door after them, then crossed the room to the writing-table and started closing its drawers, bundling papers into them anyhow.

"You mean you didn't know she'd disappeared?" Royle asked.

"No, would I have come to see her if I had?" Neville dropped into a chair near the electric fire, which was exactly the same as the one in Charlotte's cottage, then appeared to realize that he had not invited his guests to sit and waved a hand vaguely at two other chairs. His hands were slender and white. "We'd an appointment to meet here today for lunch. We'd some things to talk over. When I didn't find her I thought she must have gone out shopping and would be back any time. Now you say she's disappeared. What do you mean?"

"You mean you haven't heard about the murder?" Royle asked.

Neville's greenish eyes, with their fringes of long lashes, widened. The lashes looked very thick and dark against his pale cheeks.

"What murder?"

"You haven't heard of it?"

"No."

"Do you know a man called Edgar Frensham?"

"Of course."

"But you don't know that he was shot dead on Saturday evening?"

Neville caught his breath, then pushed a groping hand through his auburn hair.

"Frensham dead?" he said. "Then why did she want me to come here?"

"When did you make this appointment with her?" Royle asked.

"On Saturday morning. She wanted me to come down yesterday, but I was going to spend the weekend with friends in Oxford, so I said I'd look in on her on my way home today."

"So the police haven't been in touch with you yet?"

"No . . . look here, you're asking a hell of a lot of questions. What's all this got to do with you?"

Charlotte decided to take a hand. "He isn't really a

neighbour. He's a private detective. There's no need for you to answer anything if you don't want to."

Royle shot her a malignant glance, then gave a resigned shrug of his shoulders.

"Yes, that's true," he said. "But actually you asked for some information, didn't you? And I was just feeling out how much you didn't know before going ahead and telling you what you want to know. You see, Miss Cambrey, who arrived on Saturday afternoon, went up to Brickett's Farm soon after she got here and was let in by your wife, who, for reasons best known to herself, said she was Miss Sharples, who you may know is the Frenshams' housekeeper. Miss Cambrey only stayed a few minutes—that's right, isn't it?" he said, turning to Charlotte.

She nodded.

"Then when she left," he went on, "your wife passed her in a car, driving furiously, and hasn't been seen since. And a little later the real Miss Sharples came to Beech Cottage, where Miss Cambrey's staying, and told her Mr. Frensham was dead. As it turned out, he'd been shot in the head, leaving behind a rather curious suicide's letter. But there was no gun in the room. If he really committed suicide, someone went into the room after he died and took the gun away. And that could have been your wife. It's almost certain that she at least knew he was dead when Miss Cambrey saw her. She appeared to be in a state of shock."

"You've been finding out quite a lot," Charlotte muttered. "I didn't tell you all that."

"That's a part of my job," Royle said.

Marcus Neville thrust both hands through his hair, clutching his head as if it might twist or jerk in some eccentric way if he did not control it.

"Oh God!" he said. "Oh God, Isobel!"

"You believe she murdered Frensham?"

"No, no, but she took the gun, that's obvious."

"Why?"

Neville let go of his head and gave a long, agonized sigh.

"She often threatened to do it—to kill herself, you know—but I never took her seriously. People usually don't, I suppose. We all believe the old chestnut that the people who threaten to commit suicide don't do it, but it's quite untrue, of course. Sooner or later they're very likely to get around to it. And if she'd found Frensham dead . . . She was madly in love with him, you know."

"But she'd just got engaged to a young man called Ian Havershaw," Charlotte said. "Hadn't you heard about him?"

He made a gesture with one of his long hands as if he were brushing something irrelevant out of the way.

"The young man who lives in the barn? Oh yes. But she was in love with Frensham. She wanted to marry him. That's why she wanted to see me—to discuss divorce. We've been living separately for over a year, ever since she met Frensham—in fact, even before she came to live down here —but we never got around to a divorce. I told her on the telephone it was no use, I wasn't going to divorce her, but she pleaded with me to come here and talk the thing over. So I came. But it seems I was too late."

"Why wouldn't you divorce her?" Charlotte asked. "Are you a Catholic?"

"No, I was simply trying to do what I thought best for her." Neville shot an abstracted glance in her direction and added in a confused tone. "You said something about Ian Havershaw. What was it?"

"Just that he told me he and she had decided to get married."

"She didn't tell you that herself?"

"No."

"Then it probably isn't true. She'd led him up the garden

path, as she has so many others. I understand that about her, you see, and I know how badly she needs the kind of understanding I can give her. She knows it herself when she's in her right mind, and she's always turned to me when she was in trouble. And I think she knew I wouldn't divorce her for Frensham, because one of his sort could only do her harm. I decided to let her stay down here by herself till she'd got him out of her system, then fetch her home. She'd be glad to come by the time he'd done all the things to her that I knew he would."

"Where's home?" Royle asked.

"A flat in Fulham. I'm an artist. Not a very successful one, but I'm fortunate enough to have private means."

"Did she know about the other woman in his life, the one who wrote him passionate, threatening letters?"

Neville started slightly, as if he had been suddenly and sharply reminded of something that he had been trying to forget. But he shook his head.

"She never mentioned any other woman to me. But it doesn't surprise me if there is one. In fact, that's one of the things I tried to make her understand, that there was bound to be someone else sooner or later. Who is she?"

"The police still don't know," Royle answered. "But they found a number of letters from her in a safe in the house. They're all signed B, and their dates overlap with the time Frensham must have started his affair with your wife. But that's all they know about them at present."

Neville took hold of his head again, pressing his temples.

"I wonder . . ." he said. "Perhaps she knew. If she did, it might explain this so-called engagement to the man Havershaw. The rebound. An attempt to show Frensham she didn't give a damn for him." He turned to Charlotte. "I've heard about him, but I've never met him. What's he like?"

"Very young," she said. "At least five years younger than

she is. And with a lot of charm, though you'd never call him good-looking. And very much in love with her and prepared to idolize her for her impeccable honesty and integrity."

"There you are then," Neville said, lowering his hands and turning them limply outwards in a gesture of surrender. "Just what she'd want after a dose of a callous brute like Frensham. I feel sorry for the boy because, of course, she'd never have married him. In the end she'd have come back to me."

"But you think she killed herself," Royle reminded him.

Neville did not answer for some time, then he gave a deep sigh. "Perhaps not."

"What's made you change your mind?"

"Oh, only a hope that I might have been wrong. I love her very much, you see. Even if she's a murderess, I'd sooner she was alive than dead." His voice broke on the words. "And perhaps she only fled out of panic. She isn't a very rational person. She might easily lose her head."

"Where would she go if she simply bolted?"

"I don't know. I suppose there's no chance Havershaw's concealing her?" ·

"I think the police would have found her by now if he were."

"Yes, I'm sure you're right. Perhaps she's gone abroad. She might have done anything. You see, it seems to me that if there was this other woman and Isobel found Frensham was dead, she might jump to the conclusion that she was bound to be suspected because she'd got the motive of jealousy. I told you she isn't very reasonable, and she isn't very brave either. A different sort of woman would have stayed and faced it out, but not Isobel. Her first instinct would have been to hide. About that suicide letter you mentioned, what was there curious about it?"

"Several things," Royle answered. "It was in a stamped,

addressed envelope, as if he'd meant to post it before killing himself. Then its tone was strange. It read as if it had been written with some care, not by someone desperate enough to shoot himself in a few minutes. Then he talked in it of trying to kill himself in such a way as to leave as little untidiness as possible for other people to clear up, and I don't think shooting yourself in the middle of your drawing-room, so that blood gets splashed all over your excellent cream-coloured carpet, is exactly a tidy way of doing it."

"So the police think the letter was a forgery."

"No, apparently they don't. They're pretty sure the writing was Frensham's. But why he should have written a letter like that—a bit long-winded, you know, not to say verbose— is something they can't answer."

"Could it have been a joke?" Neville suggested tentatively.

"Rather a macabre one," Royle answered. "And what would have been the point of it?"

"Oh, it might have been a crude sort of hoax on the police. They'd have come rushing out to the house, and there he'd have been, fit and well. I can imagine him doing a thing like that."

"And someone who knew he'd written the letter took advantage of it to blow his brains out and probably left the gun lying beside him to help the picture of suicide along, but then your wife came and spoilt it by taking the gun away. Well, it's a possible theory."

A tide of colour suddenly washed over Marcus Neville's face. He sprang to his feet. His thin, lax body had become as taut as a coiled spring.

"Damn you and your theories!" he shouted excitedly. "Get out of here and leave me alone! I'm scared to death my wife's killed herself and you talk about possible theories!"

"I thought it was your own theory," Royle said.

Neville seemed not to hear him. "Get out of here! Leave me alone! You aren't the police, you haven't the right to ask me all these questions!"

"You're quite right, of course." Timothy Royle stood up. Seeing it, Charlotte also got to her feet. "I hope you hear from your wife soon. Good-bye."

He opened the door for Charlotte and the two of them went out into the chill, moist air of the morning.

They walked slowly down the drive and back along the main road to Beech Cottage, silent until they almost reached it.

Then Charlotte said, "I can give you lunch of a sort, if you like."

"Thanks, but don't bother," he said. "I rather want to have a talk with Havershaw."

"You know, that man isn't the least what I expected," she said. "Going by what Ian Havershaw said about him, I was expecting a tough sort of business man who believed his wife's only job in life was to further his career. I wasn't expecting that sensitive plant."

"Are you sure he's so sensitive?" Royle asked. "He may be just a rather good actor. And those delicate, nervous types can sometimes be as tough as nails. And what was he looking for in his wife's writing-table? I'd rather like to know that."

"Then do you think he knew about the murder all along and perhaps knows where she is now?"

"It wouldn't surprise me. I'd also like to know if the telephone call he had from her was really on Saturday morning, before the murder, or some time after it. He must have had a key to get into the cottage, mustn't he? That might mean he's actually seen her."

He turned to go away.

Charlotte said, "Incidentally, you're quite a bit of an actor yourself, aren't you? When I first saw you I thought you seemed quite insignificant. I'm sure you won't mind my saying that, because it's what you wanted me to think. But now I've a feeling I shouldn't like to cross you."

"No reason why you should, that I know of. Not at present." He smiled. "Will you be in later today if I should happen to drop in again?"

"I expect so. There's just one thing . . ."

"Yes?"

"I wish I knew whom you're working for. As things are, I somehow can't make up my mind how far I can trust you."

"Let's say I'm working for myself," he said. "For the money I'm paid. I need it. Do you need to know any more?"

He raised a hand in a small gesture of farewell and set off down the road.

Charlotte let herself in at her own door and set about fixing the frozen pizza that she had bought for her lunch. While it was warming up she had another drink and made some coffee. The time was two o'clock, later than she had realized. Yet she was not very hungry. She ate only about half of the pizza. She found that her talk with Timothy Royle and the admissions that she had made to him about why she had come here had got something out of her system and left her with the feeling that the only sensible thing for her to do now was to go back to London. Coming to Mattingley to seek out Edgar Frensham and persuade him to change the testimony that he had given at Dick's trial had never been a good idea, and now that he was dead there was nothing whatever to be gained by staying. If he had been a very much more dishonest citizen than he had made himself out to be at the trial and than people believed him to be, the police, with access to his safe, already knew far more about it than she did. She actually knew very little. Her faith in Dick's gentleness, in the impossibility of his ever pointing a gun at anyone, even if he was somewhat irresponsible and unstable, was all that she had to go upon.

Such matters as tracing his two supposed accomplices were quite beyond her. Those were strictly police concerns. A weary depression gripped her as she recognized how helpless she was and had been from the start. But she also felt a kind of relief that there was nothing that she could do. She felt ashamed of this feeling, yet what was it but coming to terms with reality?

She would go back to London tomorrow, she decided, unless the police objected. She would get in touch with them later in the day to find out if they did. She would go home and start looking for a new job and try to accept the fact that Dick was in prison for five years and that the best thing that she could do for him was to have some sort of home and some money, if she could save it, waiting for him when he came out. Also she must try to learn patience and kindness, of which, she thought, she had never had such a great amount, to help him face without too self-destroying a bitterness the world that had treated him with such injustice.

She wondered if Superintendent Barr was at Brickett's this afternoon or in Mattingley, and how she could find him to ask him if she might go home next day. That morning, when she had gone to the village to shop, she had noticed a public telephone on the outskirts of the village, and she thought that presently she would go along and ring up the house, and if he was not there, the police station in Mattingley. It was about four o'clock when she set out towards the telephone box. Dusk was falling already and again she felt the nip of frost in the air. The sky was a deep, clear blue in which stars were beginning to sparkle. She opened the gate and found herself face to face with Mr. and Mrs. Grainger.

They were both dressed in jeans and sheepskin jackets and in the half-light looked even more alike than they had the evening before.

"Oh, were you just going out?" Mrs. Grainger said. "Don't let us stop you then. We just called in to make sure you were all right. I don't know how you can bear it, being alone in a place like this after what's happened. But then I'm an awful coward. I can't bear being alone at night. If Ben's away for the night I always go to stay with my sister. He laughs at me about it. He says, 'What have we got worth stealing?' Or, 'D'you really think you're going to get raped and murdered just tonight of all nights?' And put like that, of course, I realize how ridiculous it sounds, but you can't change your own nature, can you? All my life I've been afraid of being left alone."

"You're talking too much," her husband said. "You haven't really said why we came here. We came to ask if you'd care to move in with us till this trouble's over. We've got a spare bedroom in our cottage, and you're very welcome to it if you'd like to come and stay. It's true Liz gets frightened when there's nothing on earth to get frightened of, but at the moment I wouldn't blame anyone for feeling scared of being alone. We know there's someone around who's already shot one person, and there's the fact that you were almost a witness of it. In fact, he might think you saw more than you did. So if you'd care to pack a few things and move in with us, you'd be very welcome."

"You're very kind," Charlotte said, pausing in the gateway. "Won't you come in? I was only going along to the telephone, but there's no hurry about it."

"If you're sure we aren't a nuisance," Mrs. Grainger said. "We won't stay a minute."

"But we mean what we said," Mr. Grainger said. "It doesn't seem right, somehow—someone young like you staying here all alone."

"It's very kind of you," Charlotte said again. She led them back into the cottage. "But I'm quite all right. And I'm thinking of going back to London tomorrow."

Inside the cottage, both Graingers undid their jackets, but did not take them off, making it clear that they really did not mean to stay long. The three of them sat down round the fire.

"That's what I'd like to do," Mrs. Grainger said. "As a matter of fact, we're thinking of moving into Mattingley. We don't like it here any more. The police, the press and morbid sight-seers, it doesn't seem—well, nice. If we could, we'd move into the flat over the shop, in spite of the mess it's in, only the contract isn't signed yet, so naturally they won't let us have the keys. But it won't be long now, and we could afford a hotel for a week or two. I'm just longing to go, although there's that awful thing that happened in Mattingley this morning. You've heard about it, I expect."

Charlotte shook her head. "I haven't heard anything."

"Well, the rumours about it may be quite untrue," Mrs. Grainger went on, "but they do say it's connected with what the police found in Mr. Frensham's safe. You really haven't heard about it?"

"No," Charlotte said.

"Mr. Entwistle's suicide?"

Charlotte shook her head again.

"Well, he was on the council and chairman of the planning committee, and the rumour is he'd been taking bribes from a firm of architects to steer a lot of business their way. And this morning he was found dead in his bed after taking a huge dose of barbiturates, and the story goes that he did it as soon as he heard of Mr. Frensham's death because he knew the police would find the evidence Mr. Frensham had been collecting against him."

"You're talking too much again," her husband said irritably. "How can you possibly know if any of that is true? You always swallow all the gossip anybody tells you. Don't take any notice of her, Miss Cambrey. It's true a Mr. Entwistle died last night—we heard it from the husband of the woman who goes in to do daily work for the Entwistles. We were having our lunch in a pub in Mattingley after going to the shop to plan a few changes we want to make, and this man started talking to us and telling us the shock it had been to his wife. And he told us the death was suicide and how no one was surprised, because everyone knew this man Entwistle had been taking bribes and was bound to be caught sooner or later. And the cleaning woman once heard Mr. Frensham threatening him. But it's Liz's own idea that what the police found in Frensham's safe had anything to do with it. Liz is always full of ideas. You want to be careful how much you believe."

She gave an exasperated but affectionate laugh.

"The things you say about me! Miss Cambrey, didn't the police tell you there was stuff in that safe of Mr. Frensham's that was absolute dynamite?"

"I think what they said to me was that it was 'interesting,'" Charlotte said.

"Well, doesn't that mean the same thing? Didn't you take it to mean it was the sort of stuff that could be used for black mail? Or if not for black mail, because after all we've no evidence that Mr. Frensham wasn't an absolutely honest and upright man, then wouldn't you have taken it to be the sort of stuff that could have been used to expose bribery and corruption and other sins, and that that's just how he'd have used it if he hadn't been cut off? I'm sure it had something to do with Mr. Entwistle's suicide."

"I'm sure it's all a coincidence," Mr. Grainger said. "It's just Liz's imagination that's linked the things. I dare say a number of people died in Mattingley last night, what with road accidents and old people going to their appointed ends and young thugs with knives and so on, it's just that we don't happen to have heard of them. Now, are you sure you won't come to stay the night with us, because you'd be truly welcome."

"It's very good of you and I do appreciate it," Charlotte said, "but I think I'll just stay here, at least until tomorrow."

Mr. Grainger stood up and tapped his wife on the shoulder.

"Come along then, Liz. We're stopping Miss Cambrey making her telephone call."

Mrs. Grainger stood up.

"But if you should change your mind later," she said, "just come along. It's the cottage beyond Birdie's—Miss Bird's, you know, where we had drinks yesterday evening. Good-bye for now."

She put an arm through her husband's and they set out into the evening, which was almost dark by now.

Charlotte shut the door behind them, then took off her jacket, uncertain suddenly if she wanted to make the call to Mr. Barr. She felt confused, as if, during the last few minutes, she had been told something important that she had already forgotten, but which it would be best to remember before deciding on any course of action. She drew the curtains and picked up her book. But when she tried to read her attention wandered. How much better it would have been if she had never come here at all. All the same, now that she was here and involved in the murder by the accident of having met Mrs. Neville just after it, wouldn't it be best to avoid giving any impression of wanting to run away? She might still try to find out more about Edgar Frensham.

For instance, she might call tomorrow on old Mrs. Frensham and see if she could get her to talk at all freely about her stepson. She might get Miss Sharples to talk about him. That ought not to be too difficult. And it might even be useful to talk more openly to the police than she had till now and see if they would respond by giving her some useful information about Frensham. It was unlikely, but it might be worth a try.

The door-knocker sounded again. She had been so lost in her thoughts that she started violently, then did not move. But whoever it was must be able to see the light through the curtains at the windows and so must know that she was there. When the knocking was repeated she got up and went to the door.

Angela Bird stood there. She was in her oyster-catcher costume, tight black jeans, white sweater and black quilted anorak. Slim and angular, she came into the room with long, delicate strides.

"I've been in Mattingley all day, working," she said. "I've only just got home and I came round to ask if anything more's been happening here. I heard a rumour that Marcus Neville has been seen here? D'you know if it's true?"

"Who told you?" Charlotte asked.

"Miss Sharples. Actually I went up to the house as soon as I got back from Mattingley to ask if Mrs. Frensham was all right or if there was anything I could do for her, and Miss Sharples said she'd been into Mattingley by bus to get some books from the library for Mrs. Frensham, and when the bus passed the end of the drive up to Jasmine Cottage she saw Marcus Neville coming out of it. At least, she was almost sure it was him. He's been down visiting Isobel a number of times since she came to live here, and Miss Sharples doesn't know anyone else who dresses in red velvet."

"Yes, he was there," Charlotte said. "He said he'd had a message from his wife saying she wanted to discuss a divorce with him. He thought it was because she wanted to marry Mr. Frensham, and he'd decided not to agree because he didn't think it would work out well for her. He didn't seem to have heard it was actually Ian Havershaw she wanted to marry, and he didn't seem much impressed by it when I told him. Do you know him well?"

"Oh no, not well. But from the little I saw of him, I thought he was a complicated, tricky sort of character."

"But you knew Mr. Frensham well, didn't you?" Charlotte said. "What did you think of him?"

Miss Bird gave her cackle of a laugh.

"Well, I told you yesterday, didn't I, he was a very easy person to dislike?" she said. "But to be honest with you, I didn't dislike him at first. He could be very charming when he chose. But you were a fool if you believed a word he said to you, and that isn't a quality I like. And he was a bully. If you didn't fall in with everything he suggested, he'd take it out on you somehow, humiliate you in front of other people, if he could, and tell slanderous stories about you. They had a nurse for Mrs. Frensham for a time called Beatrice Wallace, a stolid, conscientious creature who insisted on her authority when it came to looking after Mrs. Frensham, and he told everyone that she'd fallen madly in love with him and made a joke of it because of her unattractiveness. He always tried to make a fool of her if there was anyone there to see. I told him what I thought of him for doing it, so he turned against me, but he was always a little afraid of me and didn't try to interfere with me here."

"Had he always lived with Mrs. Frensham?" Charlotte asked.

"Oh no, only for about three years. And one of the strange things about him is that really we know very little about him. We know he came to help Mrs. Frensham run this place about three years ago and that she said he'd been farming in South Africa, but that he didn't like it any more and wanted to get away from the place. But he never talked about South Africa, so sometimes I wondered if really there was a bit of a mystery about him. Besides, I didn't think he was the kind of man to worry about colour problems and all that. In fact, I thought he was just the type to be glad to have a lot of blacks to boss. But perhaps I'm wronging him. Don't take too much notice of what I say about him. The fact is, I simply couldn't bear the man."

She zipped up her anorak, said good-night and left, lean and black and white and handsome.

She was not Charlotte's last visitor that evening. About a quarter of an hour after she had gone the door-knocker sounded again. Charlotte felt fairly sure that this time it would be Timothy Royle. He had said that he would probably drop in again. But when she opened the door it was a woman who stood there. A woman in a grey tweed coat with a high fox collar and blonde hair drawn straight back from her pale, oval face.

She started to say something. Then there was a strange noise. There was a crack and a whistle in it, something like the swish of an enormous whip. The woman made a little grunting sound, then toppled into a crumpled heap in the little porch. Blood began to seep out through her grey coat between her shoulder blades.

CHAPTER SIX

Charlotte heard the sound of running footsteps. Running away, she thought, as she stood petrified in the doorway. Then she saw lights in the road, but it was only the bus from Mattingley going by in the direction of the village. Then she realized that there were footsteps coming towards the cottage.

Panic froze her. Before those footsteps reached the gate, she must act. In a state of shock, she thrust her hands under the arms of the woman on the door-step and pulled. The body was far heavier than she had expected. It moved an inch or two, then seemed to exert extraordinary power to resist her. Behind her shone the light from the living-room and both she and what was left of the blonde woman were perfectly outlined against it as a target for whomever was coming. But at least she could turn the light off.

She reached out to the switch, but just before she turned it off, she saw Timothy Royle at the gate, with the shaft of light from the doorway falling on his face.

He came in, grasped the limp body of the woman under the arms, as Charlotte had done, slid her easily over the threshold into the cottage and slammed the door.

"It's all wrong to move her, of course," he said. "Bad for her and bad for the police. But there's someone out there with a gun and we don't want him taking pot shots at us." He felt for the heart. "Get blankets, will you, and a hot water bottle if you've got one, and turn on another bar of the fire. I think there's a chance she's still alive."

Charlotte pressed the switch of the fire, then ran upstairs. There were blankets in the second bedroom for which she had had no use and there was a hot water bottle hanging in the bathroom. She went downstairs with them, helped Royle wrap the woman on the floor in the blankets and took the hot water bottle out to the kitchen, filled the kettle and switched it on.

As she waited for it to heat, she went to the door of the living-room. The woman's face was ashen grey. Timothy Royle had thrust a cushion under her head. With the blankets swathed about her, there was no blood to be seen, but there was a long smear of it where she had been dragged across the floor from the front door to where she lay.

"She can't be alive," Charlotte said on a high note of fear.

"There's just a possibility she is," Royle answered. "I think I felt her heart. We need a doctor."

"And the police."

"Yes, but a doctor at once."

"Dr. Maynard."

"Is he somewhere near?"

"He lives in the village. I'll go and telephone him if you'll look after the kettle."

"All right."

She did not wait to put on her jacket but plunged straight out into the darkness. Then, when she was at the gate, she realized that she had not brought her handbag and that she would need coins to telephone the doctor. She dashed back into the cottage and nearly fell over a handbag that lay on the doorstep. Isobel Neville must have been carrying a bag and dropped it when she was shot.

Picking it up, Charlotte flung it down on the table and

picked up her own bag and her torch. She could hear Royle in the kitchen, filling the hot water bottle. The woman on the floor had not stirred. Charlotte found it difficult to believe that she could be alive, but she set out once more. She saw the white Renault in the road. Running till she was breathless, then walking, then running again, she came to the telephone box.

She had entered it and let the door slam behind her before it occurred to her to wonder why Royle had let her come out into the darkness in which a gunman might still be hidden, instead of offering to come himself. Perhaps it was simply because that was the kind of man he was, inclined the leave the dangerous jobs to others. Or could it be that he knew that there was no gunman out here because the only gun had been held in his own hand and that it had been madness to leave him alone with Isobel Neville, who perhaps had been alive when he had dragged her in, but would certainly be dead by the time that Charlotte returned to the cottage?

She fumbled her way through the pages of a tattered telephone directory, and found Dr. Maynard's number. When she dialled it, a woman's voice answered, cool, impersonal, distinct. His answering service, giving her the number where he was to be found that evening. Charlotte had to listen twice to the recorded message before she felt collected enough to note down the number and then dial once more. This time he answered, a little irritably at being interrupted in whatever he was doing, but he responded quickly when she told him what had happened.

"I see. Well, go back and stay with her," he said, "and I'll phone for an ambulance and the police and I'll be along myself in a few minutes. Isobel Neville—you're sure?"

"It's the woman I saw in Brickett's on Saturday evening," she answered.

"I see. I'll be along almost at once."

As the dialling tone buzzed in her ear again she put the telephone down and went breathlessly back along the road to the cottage.

Nothing had changed in it except that Timothy Royle was sitting in one of the wicker chairs, quietly going through the contents of the handbag that Charlotte had thrown down on the table. He had taken out a purse, a note-case, a fountain pen, a compact, a lipstick, a comb and a handkerchief and laid them on the floor at his feet. At the moment he was going through a small red notebook that looked like a diary.

"This is a very interesting thing," he said without looking up as Charlotte came in. "A diary for this year and there isn't a single entry in it. All the way from January to this December and there isn't one entry."

Charlotte took no notice. She was feeling very cold. Her teeth were chattering. Sitting down close to the fire, she asked, "How is she?"

"I don't know," he said. "I believe she's alive, but whether she'll last long enough for anything to be done for her, I don't know. But isn't this interesting? Why should she keep a diary in her handbag all this time if she doesn't mean to write in it?"

"Perhaps it's written in invisible ink," she answered savagely. "Tell me, how do I know you aren't the person who shot her?"

He glanced up at her, surprised. "Didn't you hear him running away?"

"I only heard you running. Where had you been?"

"Up to Brickett's. I was coming down the drive when I heard the shot and then running footsteps. By the time I got to the end of the drive, there was no one around."

"What direction did the man run away in?"

"I don't know. The bus went by just then and I couldn't hear anything. He may even have got onto it."

"You didn't see anyone?"

"I saw nothing but the bus. Tell me, do you carry a diary in your handbag?"

"Usually."

"What do you put in it?"

"Just odd appointments I might forget and sometimes expenses I want to keep a note of. Nothing much."

"But you write *something* in it?"

"Yes."

"Then don't you agree this is odd?"

"Oh, I don't know. Perhaps she lost her old one and just bought another, or perhaps she doesn't normally use a diary at all, but somebody gave her this as a present and she felt she had to carry it about to be polite. Mr. Royle . . ."

"My name's Timothy," he said as she paused. "But please not Tim. I had some friends with a fox-terrier when I was a child called Tim, and it's always seemed to me a dog's name."

"I don't think it matters what we call one another," she said. "Our relationship hasn't progressed to the point where it's of any significance."

"What long words you use," he said.

She felt a danger that she might choke on a sob. "How can you—how *can* you?" she said. "There's someone lying there dead or dying and you make silly jokes."

"I'm sorry," he said. "It's a way disaster often takes me. I take refuge in a dreadful flippancy. What were you going to say?"

"You said you were coming down the drive from Brickett's when you heard the shot."

"Yes, I was coming to see you."

"What were you doing at Brickett's?"

"Oh, asking a few questions about this and that," he said.

"Isn't it the fact that Mrs. Frensham's your client?"

He stooped, picking up the objects that he had laid out on the floor and scooping them back into the handbag that he was holding. She could not see his face.

"I wonder what gave you that idea," he said.

"It's a way you could have found out all the things you know," she said. "You know all about what was in that safe. Mrs. Frensham could have told you that, once she'd got it from the police."

"But what do you imagine an old woman like her could possibly want with the services of a detective?" He raised his head and looked up at her. He was wearing his nondescript face again, the face of deadly ordinariness that told her nothing. She wondered how it was possible that at times she had almost thought him good-looking.

"She may have wanted to know a little more about that stepson of hers than she did," she answered. "She *is* your client, isn't she? You haven't denied it."

"I hardly ever deny anything," he said. "Once you start you may go on doing it till you're driven into a corner where there's only one thing left to say and you have to admit that's the truth. Or else you have to admit you've been telling lies all along and that's distasteful. About the diary—"

"Damn the diary!"

The gate squeaked.

"There's Dr. Maynard," she said, jumped to her feet and went to the door.

Dr. Maynard came in wearing his tweed overcoat and felt hat, with his round, friendly face full of concern, but betraying no sign of his having hurried since Charlotte's telephone call. He took off his hat and coat and laid them on a chair before advancing to the prone figure of the woman on the floor. Then, drawing back the blankets with which she had been covered, he knelt beside her and felt her pulse, then felt for her heart-beat. Then he sat back on his heels, covering her again with the blankets.

"It's Isobel Neville," he said. "You were right about that."

"Is she alive?" Charlotte asked tensely.

"Just," he answered. "If we can get her to the hospital in time, we may pull her through. The bullet obviously missed her heart, but I'm not sure where it's gone. I think the ambulance will be here any minute now. Do you know what brought her here?"

"No," Charlotte said. "She came to the door and knocked and then, just as I opened it, someone shot at her and she collapsed in the doorway. She didn't have a chance to say a word to me."

"And you brought her in here by yourself?" He looked at Royle. "Or did this gentleman help?"

Charlotte remembered that to the best of her knowledge the doctor and the detective had not met yet.

"He helped," she said. "He says he was coming down the drive from Brickett's when he heard the shot. His name's Timothy Royle and he's a detective. If you ask him whom he's working for, he won't tell you, but I believe it's Mrs. Frensham."

Dr. Maynard got to his feet.

"You're a detective?" he said to Royle.

"That's correct," Royle answered.

"Working with the police?"

"Hardly that. I arrived in Mattingley before there'd even been a murder."

"But you know a good deal, I expect, about what's been going on."

"Not as much as I'd like."

"Naturally. We're all in the dark. But you know about the safe, I suppose, and perhaps something about what was in it."

"To the best of my knowledge, there wasn't much in it," Royle replied. "Some letters from an infatuated woman, a few other documents, nothing else."

"Those documents," the doctor said. "I wonder what they were."

"The police haven't told me anything about them."

"Nor Mrs. Frensham either?"

"Mrs. Frensham is a very old woman," Royle said. "Ninety-four, I believe. If they did tell her anything, she may not have understood it."

Charlotte recognized one of his evasions. He had neither denied nor admitted anything.

"Of course, of course," Dr. Maynard said. "But I can tell you one thing—Mrs. Frensham is a lot more astute than a lot of people twenty years younger than she is. It wouldn't surprise me if she knew all about what was in that safe. She's told you nothing about it, however?"

"Why should she? I didn't tell you I was working for her, did I?"

"No, that was Miss Cambrey. All the same . . ." Dr. Maynard looked searchingly at Royle's unrevealing face. "Well, this isn't the time to be talking about such matters, but I'd like to know . . . no, it doesn't matter. But if you'd come and see me sometime, I might make it worth your while. I'm interested in that safe." He turned his head to listen. "That's the ambulance, I think."

But it was not the ambulance, it was the police, Superintendent Barr, the sergeant and two constables. The ambulance arrived a few minutes later. Isobel Neville was carefully lifted onto a stretcher and carried away. Dr. Maynard, who had exchanged a few words with the Superintendent,

went with her, while Mr. Barr, sending the constables to
wait outside and settling his bulk in one of the wicker
chairs, asked to be told the events of the evening.

Charlotte told him of hearing the door-knocker, of
finding herself facing Isobel Neville, of the sound of the
shot and the blonde woman's collapse and Timothy Royle's
arrival a moment later. Mr. Barr glanced at Royle when she
mentioned his name, then back at Charlotte, subjecting her
to his wide, formidable stare.

"So she didn't tell you why she came to see you," he said.

"She hadn't time," she answered.

"Why do you think she came?"

"I haven't any idea."

"You'd met her just once?"

"Yes, that evening at Brickett's."

"Are you sure of that? You'd never met her on any other
occasion, in London, perhaps?"

"I've told you that already," Charlotte said flatly. "I saw
her for just those few minutes on Saturday evening when
she pretended to be Miss Sharples."

"Ah, yes. And we don't know why she did that, do we?
Have you any thoughts about it?"

"All I can think of is that she was very frightened at having been found there just after she'd stumbled on Mr. Frensham's body in the drawing-room, and she wanted above all
things to get away without having to explain what she was
doing there. We don't know what she was doing there, do
we?"

"No, I can't say we do, though Mr. Havershaw believes
she'd gone to the house to tell Mr. Frensham she was going
to marry him and put an end to her affair with Mr. Frensham. But we've no evidence that that was the case. I understand, however, you've decided in your own mind she

stumbled on Mr. Frensham's dead body, as you put it, and wasn't herself the murderess."

"Someone tried to murder her this evening, didn't they?" Charlotte said. "Do you think there's a second murderer in the neighbourhood?"

He put the tips of his long, powerful fingers together and looked at her over the top of them.

"That can happen, you know," he said. "That can very easily happen. One thing leads to another. People imitate one another. Still, we don't know yet why she disappeared, do we, or why she came back? What was she so frightened of that she felt she had to disguise her identity and vanish? Could it have been you, Miss Cambrey?"

"I don't know what you mean," Charlotte said.

"Suppose the name Cambrey meant something to her."

"What could it have meant?"

"Oh, come," he said. "We know Mr. Frensham was a principal witness recently at your brother's trial at the Old Bailey, and Cambrey isn't a particularly common name. He must have known who you were when he let the cottage to you. It would be interesting to know just why he agreed to do that, in the circumstances, but no doubt he had his reasons, just as you had yours for coming here. He may simply have wanted to know what you were going to try to do. But the chances are that if he and Mrs. Neville were intimate, he'd have told her what he'd done and who you were and when she saw you she leapt to the conclusion that you'd got to the house before her and done the murder. As perhaps you had, Miss Cambrey."

He leant forward, putting a hand on each thick knee in a disturbingly threatening gesture.

Timothy Royle, who had been standing leaning against the half-empty bookcase in the corner, came forward and stood in front of Mr. Barr.

"If you're going to talk like that," he said, "don't you think Miss Cambrey should have a solicitor?"

"Certainly, certainly, if she wants one," Mr. Barr said urbanely. "But we're only talking hypothetically, I thought that was understood. I haven't even suggested she should come to the police station to make a statement. I'd be the first to agree that if Mrs. Neville ran away from Miss Cambrey on Saturday evening because she thought she was a murderess, it's strange she should have come to her this evening. But Miss Cambrey seems to see so many things happen and there's no one to corroborate any of it. She says she sees Mrs. Neville at Brickett's Farm on Saturday—but does she? She says Mrs. Neville came here and was shot from behind before they had time to exchange a word—but was she? Suppose she'd been in here for some time and was shot from behind as she was leaving. Again there's no one to say that isn't how it happened."

"There is," Royle said angrily. "I was here. I arrived only a moment after it happened. Miss Cambrey was trying to drag Mrs. Neville into this room, but she was too heavy for her and I had to help. And from the sound of the shot I knew it had come from outside and I heard footsteps running away."

Mr. Barr nodded his massive head. "Well, that's something, though the direction of sounds can be very deceptive. And do you actually know anything about the way a body falls when it's shot either from in front or behind? By the time Dr. Maynard got here you'd already moved Mrs. Neville, so he couldn't tell us anything. But you can say, I suppose, whether she was extended over the threshold, or more in a sort of crumpled heap."

"A crumpled heap, I suppose," Royle said unwillingly.

"There you are then," Mr. Barr said. "The shot could have come from either direction."

"So your theory is that Miss Cambrey went to Brickett's on Saturday night," Royle said, "shot Mr. Frensham, was seen by Mrs. Neville, who pretended—out of panic—she hadn't seen anything, bolted, took a couple of days to think things over and then, knowing Miss Cambrey was armed and already a murderess, came along here for a nice chat."

"Oh, Mr. Royle, you're going a great deal too fast for me," Mr. Barr said in a tone that had an undercurrent of mockery in it. "I haven't a theory of any kind yet. I'm only pointing out possibilities. I'm sure Miss Cambrey understands that. But that reminds me, Miss Cambrey, have you any objection if we search this cottage now? You can refuse. I've no search warrant. But I could easily obtain one, and yesterday you actually invited us to make a search."

"Go ahead," Charlotte said.

"But this is outrageous!" Royle exclaimed. "You've no reason—"

"It's all right," Charlotte said. "I really don't mind. But you'll remember, won't you, Mr. Barr, that I ran up the road to the telephone, so I could easily have thrown the gun away in the bushes on the way there."

"I seem to detect a note of irony in those words," he observed. "Very well, we'll go ahead. And thank you for your helpfulness. You'll find it to your advantage in the long run."

He turned to the sergeant and instructed him to bring in the two constables who had been sitting in a car at the gate and proceed with the search of the cottage.

It did not take long. There was so little furniture in it and Charlotte had brought so little luggage with her that there were very few places where a gun could be concealed. But sitting in the living-room, listening to the heavy footsteps moving here and there upstairs, Charlotte found herself settling into a chilly kind of rigidity. She felt shivery with dread and unable to move. For suppose the men found something? It seemed impossible that they should, and yet the longer that she had to wait, the more convinced she became that their probing hands, emptying this and turning over that, would chance on some piece of evidence, not necessarily a gun, that would be disastrous to her. Evidence, as she knew only too well, could be a lying, misleading deception. But in the end they told Mr. Barr that they had found nothing. He did not seem surprised. Thanking Charlotte again for her helpful attitude, the four policemen departed.

"And now," Timothy Royle said when their car doors had slammed and the car had driven away, "what you need is a drink. You look ready to drop."

"I'm frightened," Charlotte said.

"I don't think you should be. What they were doing was just routine."

"Isn't that what they always say?"

"They've no evidence at all against you. And my impression of Barr is that he's a fair man, even if he doesn't know how to be genial. He won't try to trap you. Now what about some whisky?"

"I suppose it would be a good idea. I'm not really very fond of it."

"There's nothing better in a crisis."

"No." She began to get up. "I expect you'd like some too."

He put a hand on her shoulder, pressing her back into her chair.

"You stay here. I'll get it. Just try to relax. I'm afraid you aren't used to this kind of thing."

"To having corpses fall over my doorstep and being suspected of murder? I'll be honest with you, it's never happened to me before."

"Well then, take it quietly and don't worry." He disappeared into the kitchen. She heard the clink of glasses, then after a minute he returned with a drink for each of them. "I wonder if that woman's going to die, or if they'll pull her through?"

Charlotte sipped her drink. It was only as the warmth of it went through her that she realized all of a sudden how much she needed it.

"Don't let's go on and on talking about it," she said. "Let's talk about something quite different. Tell me about your wife."

"My wife?"

"Yes."

"What—what do you want to know about her?"

"Well, to begin with, what's her name?"

It was almost as if, for a moment, he found it difficult to remember. Then he said, "Mary."

"What does she look like?"

"Oh well, you know, kind of pretty—very pretty."

"Dark or fair?"

"Sort of in between."

"Tall or short?"

"Just about medium."

"You aren't very eloquent about her. "

"Well, you know how it is, it's difficult to describe someone you know very well."

"I suppose with five children to look after she hasn't got time to go out to a job of any kind."

"No, of course not. She just does the cooking and so on. She's a splendid cook."

"What did she do before she married you?"

He gave her a harassed look, as if he felt that he was being driven into a corner. "She was—she was a secretary."

"The funny thing is," Charlotte said, "when I saw you first, you didn't strike me at all as looking like a family man. You looked to me like someone rather under-nourished, who eats too many bad meals in cheap restaurants, not someone who's cherished by a splendid cook. I suppose your work keeps you away from home a good deal."

"Yes, of course. I've a lot of experience of those cheap restaurants you mention. Not that any of them are so very cheap nowadays. But why don't we talk about you? Have you got a job, and if so, how did you get the time off to come down here?"

"No, tell me some more about yourself. How did you become a detective?"

"That's what it's said men always ask the tarts they go with. How did you get into the game? Do you feel it's a particularly disreputable kind of job then, being a detective?"

"It could be, I suppose. I should think it's a case of what you make of it."

"That's just about the truth. Well, I was out of a job—I'd been in an advertising office, after a number of other things, but the agency folded—so I was ready to take on more or less anything that came along."

"Having all those ever-open mouths to feed."

"What? Oh—oh yes, them. But you're forgetting family allowances. I believe if you can produce enough children the allowances mount up so wonderfully that you can sit back and not do another stroke of work in your life. But I think it has to be twelve or thereabouts."

"Five isn't enough?"

"Definitely not. But of course I hadn't got all five of them at that time, only Deborah and Vanessa and Judy."

"I thought Judy was the youngest—the one who likes to telephone."

"Did I say that? Oh no, Sarah's the youngest."

"I don't think you happened to mention a Sarah before. Did you just forget her?"

"No, but I get confused with so many to remember. When I want one of the girls I sometimes have to call out one name after another before I hit the right one. But about my job, as I was telling you, I was just about ready to try anything when I met an old friend who was working for Hargreave's, and he told me they were looking for a man and that they'd probably take me on if I felt like trying it. I'd no training, of course, and there was a lot to learn, but by degrees I picked it up and the fact is, it's got a good deal of fascination for me now."

"And I expect you found you'd a natural talent for the work," Charlotte said.

"Honestly, I'm not sure that I have," he said. "I don't think I'm a very good detective."

"But that trick you have of being able to disguise yourself as totally, unnoticeably commonplace—it can't be everyone who can do that, and it must come in wonderfully useful sometimes."

"I'm glad you think it's a trick and not just the personality I was born with," he said. "It's very difficult to be sure of a thing like that about oneself. Sometimes I look in the mirror and say to myself, 'There's the most completely commonplace face I ever saw.' But even if it is, you're right, of course, it's a professional asset. Now let's get back to your job. You've got one, I imagine."

"I had one till my old general died," she answered. "He was writing the history of his family and I was his secretary and research assistant and did my best to keep his spirits up. His wife died about ten years ago and since that this history seemed to be the only thing that kept him going. The work was awfully dull and that might have been why he couldn't keep his secretaries for long—he'd had two or three before

me, and I'm not sure how much longer I could have stuck it
—but he was such a sweet, gentle old thing and I miss him
ever so much more than I would have expected. And I
haven't started thinking yet about what job to look for next.
You know why I came down here. But that hasn't worked
out exactly as I expected."

"I suppose, after what's happened tonight, they won't let
you go back to London tomorrow," he said.

"No." Their talk and the whisky had done Charlotte
good. She felt more relaxed than she had all day. "Do you
think she'll recover?"

"I'm sorry, I don't know much about that sort of thing.
Dr. Maynard talked as if she had a chance."

"If she doesn't recover, we'll never know why she came
to see me, shall we?"

"You really haven't any idea?"

"No, except that it must have had something to do with
our meeting on Saturday."

"Or our meeting with her husband this morning."

"Do you think he and she had been in touch?"

"I'd say that's almost certain. He went to the cottage to
find something for her. I wish I knew what."

"Could it have been the gun?"

He considered it, then shook his head.

"I don't think so. If she'd killed Frensham and left, taking the gun away with her, she wouldn't have put it carefully away in her cottage before disappearing. It would have
gone with her, wherever she went. No, it's something else,
and I've a queer feeling I almost know what it is—though
the thing eludes me. But I think it's one of the most important things we've to ask ourselves at the moment, that and
why Mrs. Neville came to see you. And also why there are
no entries in that diary of hers."

"Were you telling the truth when you said you didn't know what was in the safe?" Charlotte asked.

He leant his head back, staring up at the ceiling and did not answer.

A silence settled between them. It was unexpectedly peaceful and comfortable and Charlotte found herself unwilling to break it. She had listened to far too much talking for her own liking in the last few days. Her head buzzed with it. Silence now, in the company of this odd but apparently kindly man, was as soothing as a cool hand on her forehead.

But suddenly he looked at his watch and got to his feet.

"I must be going," he said. "There's a bus into Mattingley in a few minutes. But I can give you a piece of advice if you like. Go to see Mrs. Frensham tomorrow. I think she can tell you a good many things you want to know."

"So you *are* working for her," Charlotte said.

"As a matter of fact, no. But ask her about that and see what she says. But remember her age. Her point of view about a number of things may be peculiar. Well, goodnight, and I hope you don't run into any more murders."

He let himself out into the dark little garden.

Charlotte sat where she was for a little while. Now that she was alone she realized that the buzzing in her head was continuing. It sounded not unlike the hum of a refrigerator, but she knew that it was only nervous exhaustion. She had had it off and on ever since the day when Dick had been arrested. She thought of having another drink, then thought that it might actually make the buzzing worse. Closing her eyes, she tried to pretend that she was back in her flat in Maida Vale and not in this ill-omened cottage.

But when she closed her eyes she seemed to hear the tramping of police boots around her, in the kitchen and overhead. She had never before experienced such an invasion of her privacy as she had that evening. Even when she had been questioned about Dick, the detectives had sat quietly talking to her in her sitting-room. But now she had a feeling that all her belongings here, few though they were, had been ravished. It struck her that this must be how people often feel after a burglary. The police had been tidier and more considerate than burglars, but all the same, they had thrust their strangers' hands into the intimacies of her life and left her with a sense of having been degraded.

It was not a rational feeling. She recognized that a search could hardly have been avoided and that the sooner it was over, the better. But the comfort of the little cottage had been destroyed.

There was fear too. A murder, or an attempted murder had been committed on her door-step and was going to haunt her all night. She considered packing a suitcase, catching the next bus into Mattingley and going to a hotel.

Then all of a sudden she remembered the Graingers. They had guessed how she would feel, alone here, even before Isobel Neville had crumpled bleeding on her threshold, and they had been sincere in their invitation and would not be horrified if she appeared at their door.

Running upstairs, she bundled a nightdress and a few toilet things together and set off along the road to Rose Cottage.

The white Renault, she noticed, was gone, removed, she supposed, by the police.

CHAPTER SEVEN

The Graingers greeted her with little clucking sounds of welcome. Mrs. Grainger said that she had had a feeling that Charlotte would be round and wanted to know if she had remembered to eat anything that evening. Charlotte admitted that she had not. Very well, Mrs. Grainger said, there was the left-over of a shepherd's pie that she and Ben had had that evening, which she could warm up in no time, and some nice carrots and some stewed apples and custard. And while she was making these things ready, Ben could give Charlotte a drink. She let the drink be pressed into her hand before she remembered that she had already drunk as much as she was used to, but she felt that it would be unmannerly to refuse it.

The room was a typical suburban room of the thirties, papered in cream, grown dingy with the passing of time, furniture of fumed oak and leatherette armchairs with worn brown velvet cushions. There was a gaudily tiled fireplace in which a log fire burned. The Graingers appeared to have tried to brighten the room up with pots of plastic chrysanthemums, but in spite of the fire the room was full of draughts from the flimsy, ill-fitting doors.

"I'll keep you company," Mr. Grainger said, helping himself to a drink and sitting down facing Charlotte in one of the brown armchairs. "We saw you'd a lot of coming and going at your place this evening, with the police, the ambulance and all, and we thought perhaps we ought to come round and see if we could help, then we thought it would probably look just like curiosity and we'd only be in the way. I tell you, we were glad to see you just now, because at first we were sure the ambulance had come for you. And now don't say a word, if you'd sooner not, but we can't help wondering who was taken ill."

"I'm not sure if you can call it being taken ill," Charlotte said, "being shot in the back, but that's what happened to Mrs. Neville. She came to see me and someone shot her from the road and she collapsed on my doorstep."

"Good Lord," he said, taking hold of his lower lip and tugging at it. "Good Lord. And she's dead too, is she?"

"We don't know yet," Charlotte answered. "Dr. Maynard seemed to think there was a chance of saving her."

"Good Lord." He looked amazed and appalled. Then he raised his voice. "Liz—Liz, did you hear that?"

Mrs. Grainger put her head in from the kitchen. "What is it, dear? I'm busy."

"It's just that Miss Cambrey's been telling me about the police and all that. It was Mrs. Neville. She came to see Miss Cambrey and someone shot her in the back and they took her away in an ambulance and they don't know whether she's going to live or die."

"Oh, no!" Mrs. Grainger exclaimed. "Is that really true, dear? How terrible! Not that I'm altogether surprised somehow. That woman was always asking for trouble. I wonder where her husband was when it happened. You know, I saw him only a few times and never cared for him much, he just wasn't our sort, but I had a good deal of sympathy with him, the way she went on. Now I must go and see to the pie. I don't want it to spoil."

She disappeared into the kitchen again.

"Do you know why Mrs. Neville came to see you?" Mr. Grainger asked.

Charlotte shook her head. "That's what everyone wants to know." She wished that she had not accepted her drink, but she felt afraid of putting it down. Then all of a sudden she remembered that she had not brought her dressing-gown with her and in the draughtiness of the house she thought that she would probably be glad of it. She got to her feet. "I'm awfully sorry," she said, "but there's something I didn't bring with me. Do you mind if I just run back and fetch it while your wife's getting my supper. I'll only be two or three minutes."

"Go, of course, if that's what you want to do," he said, "but can't I do it for you? Give me your key and tell me where the thing is, then you needn't go out again. You're looking out on your feet."

"It's just my dressing-gown," she said. "You might not be able to find it. But I could go later, if that's more convenient. You're both being so kind."

"Oh, that's all right," he said. "But I'll come with you. It doesn't sound like the sort of night for you to be wandering about by yourself." He raised his voice again. "Liz, we're just going back to Beech Cottage for a few minutes to fetch something Miss Cambrey forgot."

"Well, don't be long," Mrs. Grainger called back. "Things are almost ready."

He helped Charlotte into her jacket once more, opened the door for her and they set out together.

He had brought a torch and stepped along briskly, following its cone of light, which lit up the damp green of the grass on the verge and the puddles in the road.

"Cold," he observed. "I shouldn't wonder if we have frost by the morning. A shot, you said. You're really sure that poor woman was shot? It wasn't a heart-attack, or something like that?"

"There isn't any doubt about it at all," Charlotte answered.

"How extraordinary. And it happened before she could even explain why she'd come. There must be a maniac about. Unless, of course, as Liz said, it was Mr. Neville. Liz has a way of being right about all kinds of things. I've a great trust in her intuition. All the same . . . no, I'm inclined to believe in a maniac. You've only to read the papers to realize how many of them there are about. The country's degenerating, that's my opinion. We're too soft with all these lunatics, treat them as if they were harmless invalids, don't care at all about their victims—God, what's that?"

He stood stock still, the beam of his torch wavering erratically until it focused on the gate of Beech Cottage.

The gate had just given the characteristic squeak that Charlotte had come to know as two figures came through it from the garden. She had been so startled by the abruptness of Mr. Grainger's reaction that for a moment she felt her heart beating furiously. But then she recognized her visitors as Angela Bird and Ian Havershaw.

"Oh, there you are," Miss Bird said. In her black clothes, with her black hair and white face, she looked very thin and shadowy in the dark. "Ian and I just met here. We both came to see if you were all right after all that police coming and going. What was it all about?"

"If you want to hear all about it, come back with us and she'll tell you what happened," Mr. Grainger said. "It's too cold to stand about out here, talking. Miss Cambrey's staying the night with us. We just came back to fetch something she's forgotten." He turned to her. "Run in and get what you want, but don't be too long. Liz won't be pleased with us if we keep her waiting."

"There was an ambulance," Ian Havershaw said, his

large teeth gleaming in the narrow beam of light from the torch. "I heard the siren. So when we couldn't find you here, we thought it must have been for you. Who was it for?"

"Mrs. Neville," she answered as she went through the gate, slipped her key into the lock and let herself into the cottage.

She heard him make an inarticulate sound, then realized that he had followed her in and as she started up the stairs to the bedroom was pounding up them after her.

He grasped her arm. "What did you say?"

"It was Mrs. Neville," she said, then as he held her with his long, horse-like face only a few inches from hers, she once more told the story of the evening.

He had let her go before she finished and had drawn a step back. An excitement that had lit up his face when he had first heard the name of Isobel Neville had gradually died out of it.

"You mean there isn't much hope?" he said. "She's done for?"

"Oh, I don't think so," she answered. "They seemed to think she'd a chance."

"That's what they always say, isn't it, till it's all over? They never tell you the truth."

"But I think they meant it, I really do," she said.

He gave her a dazed look, then said oddly, "I'm sorry—I mean, I'm sorry I made you break the bad news. It's a horrible thing to have to do. They're taking her to the Infirmary, I suppose. "

From downstairs Mr. Grainger's voice called up, "Are you two coming down? Liz really won't like it if we keep her waiting."

"I think it was the Infirmary," Charlotte said.

"Then I'll go there now," Ian said. "At once."

"They won't let you see her, you know."

"No, but I can wait there till there's some definite news, can't I? They won't mind that."

"Have you got a car?"

"Yes."

"Good luck, then."

He raced downstairs as she went into the bedroom, bundled her dressing-gown under her arm and followed him down.

By the time that she reached the gate, he had gone. Miss Bird and Mr. Grainger were still there, talking in low voices. It seemed that he had told her what had happened that evening. The three of them set off together down the road, but when they reached the gate of Miss Bird's cottage she paused, then said that she would go in and not trouble the Graingers further that evening. She put a hand lightly on Charlotte's shoulder, seemed about to say something, then changed her mind and went into the cottage.

Charlotte and Mr. Grainger went on to Rose Cottage and when they entered the living-room, found the table set with a red-and-white plastic cloth, knives and forks, a roll and butter and a glass of water.

"Good, everything's just ready," Mrs. Grainger said. "You'll feel better when you've had a meal. Come and sit down. You were longer than I expected."

"We met Ian and Birdie," Mr. Grainger said, "and they wanted to know what all the commotion was about. I asked them both in, but Ian went off to get his car and drive straight off to the Infirmary, and as I'd told Birdie what had happened, she decided to go home. Just as well for Miss Cambrey, I should think. She must have had just about as much fussing over as she can stand."

"As soon as she's eaten, she can go straight to bed," Mrs.

Grainger said. "It's a very plain supper you're getting, dear, but it'll do you good."

She returned to the kitchen and reappeared after a moment with a large plateful of shepherd's pie and a dish of carrots.

Charlotte sat down at the table and felt mildly uncomfortable because both Graingers sat down at the table too and appeared to be watching with deep interest every forkful of mince and potato that she lifted to her mouth, but she managed to eat what she had been given. At first she had no appetite, yet Mrs. Grainger was right, it increased as she ate and she began to feel better.

As she ate, Mrs. Grainger observed, "D'you know, an interesting thing—I'm sure I saw Nurse Wallace in Mattingley this morning."

"I thought she was in Madeira," Mr. Grainger said. "Didn't she go there with that old couple who needed a nurse to go along with them?"

"That's what I thought," Mrs. Grainger said, "but I swear I saw her today, coming out of the White Horse Hotel and she had an arm in a sling. So perhaps she had an accident and couldn't look after the old people and had to come home."

"If so, she'll try to get your cottage back from you, Miss Cambrey," Mr. Grainger said. "She was very attached to it."

"My name's Charlotte," she said.

He smiled and repeated after her, "Charlotte."

"It was her right arm she had in a sling," Mrs. Grainger went on. "D'you know, I've had such an interesting idea about her. You know all those letters in the safe the police told us about, signed B. Well, Nurse Wallace's name is Beatrice, isn't it? So she could have written them, that's what I think. But the police aren't going to be able to compare the handwriting of the letter with hers if she can't use her right

hand, so they'll have to look for something else she's written. I wonder if they'll find anything. She was terribly in
love with Mr. Frensham for a time, you know, although I
always thought he treated her abominably. But it didn't
seem to put her off. I remember the way she used to simper
at him. She was very thick-skinned. And not attractive,
poor thing. You could hardly expect him to fall for her. But
I've been wondering if those letters came from Madeira and
got more and more threatening when he wouldn't answer
them. The police said some of them were threatening, didn't
they? Don't you think I may be right?"

"Gossip," Mr. Grainger said. "Just your usual sort of
gossip. You're a dangerous woman, Liz. You ought to learn
to control your imagination."

"But you've said yourself, I'm so often right," she said.
"You've said you'd sooner trust my intuition than the evidence of your own eyes."

"That was just a manner of speaking," he answered. "I
was probably making a joke."

"You weren't, you meant it. And there's something else
about Nurse Wallace. She'd lived in that house. She knew
everything about it. If she wanted to stop the lift working so
that Mrs. Frensham couldn't come downstairs while she was
murdering Mr. Frensham, she'd have known all about how
to do it." Mrs. Grainger jumped to her feet, reaching for
Charlotte's empty plate. "There, I can see you're feeling
better already."

She trotted out to the kitchen, returning in a minute with
a plate of stewed apples and custard.

Mr. Grainger was chewing a thumb-nail as Mrs.
Grainger sat down again at the table.

"Don't take any notice of us, Charlotte," he said. "Liz
doesn't mean a quarter of what she ways. Let's have some
coffee now, Liz, before you start trying to put it into our

heads that it was Mrs. Frensham who wrote poor old Edgar those letters. You're capable of anything."

She giggled and retired to the kitchen once more.

When they had had coffee, they all went up to bed. Charlotte's sleep was broken until nearly morning, when she drifted into a deep sleep, from which she woke only when Mrs. Grainger came into her bedroom with her breakfast on a tray. There was tea, a boiled egg and toast and marmalade. It was nine o'clock.

"Here you are, dear," Mrs. Grainger said. "I didn't want to wake you, you looked so tired last night, but Ben and I have an appointment with our lawyer in Mattingley this morning, so we've got to go out now. Don't get up till you feel like it and do stay on here as long as you want. We're so glad to have you. We'll be back sometime in the afternoon, I expect. I left a key on the kitchen table in case you want to go out and come in again. Do make yourself at home. The water's hot if you want a bath. Good-bye for now."

She made sure the tray was comfortably settled on Charlotte's knees, then flitted out.

Charlotte was still drowsy and ate her breakfast slowly, drinking three cups of tea, then very nearly fell asleep again. But deciding that it was time to rouse herself, she put the tray aside, got out of bed, and thinking that a bath was a good idea, wandered yawning into the bathroom and turned on the taps. She found that a good many of the events of the day before had retreated into a foggy haze. It looked hazy outside too, with a grey-white mist lapping against the window-panes. She heard the front door open and close as the Graingers went out and the sound of their car as they drove away.

Dressing after her bath, her mind gradually cleared. She could remember everything about the day before now, some of the events coming to her with a definition that they had not had when they happened. Superintendent Barr's suspicion of her, for instance. Yesterday she had hardly been able to believe in it. Now it seemed to her very reasonable that he should look at her askance. That search of her cottage had not been mere routine. Those men had really been looking for the gun that had killed Edgar Frensham and perhaps Isobel Neville too. Charlotte wondered if the blonde woman had survived the night and whether—if she went to the public telephone on the edge of the village and called the Infirmary, they would tell her if she was alive or dead.

But when she had dressed and was ready to go out, it was not towards the village that she turned, but up the drive to Brickett's Farm.

The morning was dankly cold. The mist was light, but seemed to brush against her face with clammy fingers. The gravel of the drive squelched under her feet as she walked. Once or twice she looked behind her. If the police believed that she was a murderess it seemed normal that they should be keeping a watch on her and have left someone to follow her. But there was no one there. It started her doubting that they had any suspicions of her at all and swinging between a belief that they had and one that they hadn't, confusion came back and she began to wonder what on earth, among other things, was bringing her to Brickett's now.

Really she knew the answer to that question, but it hardly seemed good enough. But having committed herself to the visit, the stubbornness in her make-up prevented her from turning back. Reaching the door, she rang the bell.

As she did so, she noticed with a start that the door was a few inches open. It gave her an eerie feeling of being caught in a web of events that had already happened. She had a feeling that things were about to repeat themselves and that she was to be given a chance to understand something that she had totally missed before. However, things did not repeat themselves. The door was opened by a round-faced, elderly woman in an overall, who was manipulating a vacuum cleaner in the hall. The door was open simply because she had not closed it after sweeping the door-step. When Charlotte asked if she could see Mrs. Frensham, the woman looked doubtful, and as if she did not like the responsibility of showing anyone into the presence of the lady of the house, went away and returned after a moment with Miss Sharples.

The housekeeper was wearing her grey jersey dress with the neat white collar and the pink bedroom slippers that she favoured for indoor wear. Her grey hair, which had been blown into elf-locks when Charlotte had seen her last, was parted in the middle and rolled up into a neat little bun.

"Oh, it's you, dear," she said, taking one of Charlotte's hands and giving it a reassuring little pat. "Goodness, how cold you are! Don't you ever wear gloves? You know, I've been wondering about you and whether I should see how you were getting along. But she's been giving me a lot of trouble. Every time I start doing something, she shouts at me about something I'm to do immediately for her. My belief is, she can't bear being left alone, even for a little while. She doesn't seem to be exactly grieving for Mr. Edgar, but she wants attention all the time in a way she never has before. There now . . ." She cocked her head, listening. "Did you hear that?"

Charlotte had heard a shrill old voice call out, "Emily—where the bloody hell have you got to, woman? When are you bringing our coffee?"

Miss Sharples smiled with a kind of glee, as if, perhaps for the first time, she was experiencing power.

"That's how it goes all the time," she said. "But come

along, dear. She'll be glad to see you, even if she does snap your head off. Just try to understand the poor old thing. She's got no one to count on now but me, and I think that frightens her, though she's got no reason to believe I won't take good care of her. I'll never leave her as long as she needs me and I've told her so, but I'm not sure she believes me."

She led the way to one of the doors opening off the hall and thrust it open.

It led into a room that Charlotte had not seen before, a small, pretty room that was probably known as the morning-room, decorated in pale yellows, with a few comfortable chairs in flowered covers and a log fire burning in the grate. On the mantelpiece above it was a photograph of a man in a silver frame. For a moment Charlotte took him for Edgar Frensham, then she realized that this man had been at least sixty when the photograph was taken. He must be Edgar Frensham's father, an even handsomer man than his son, with an impressive air of authority about him. If he had had as strong a will as the photograph suggested, it was easy to wonder what kind of relationship had existed between him and his second wife, whom it was impossible to imagine as readily accepting domination.

She was sitting in one of the flowery chairs, dressed as she had been on Saturday evening in a purple quilted dressing-gown and diamond ear-rings and with her feet in black, beaded slippers. Her aluminium crutches were propped against one arm of her chair. She was not alone in the room. A big woman of about forty with a broad, heavy face, short, straight brown hair cut in a thick fringe across her forehead, round blue eyes and a rather loose-looking mouth was seated in one of the other chairs. She was wearing a checked tweed suit that was too tight for her, so that the skirt had ridden up, showing her thick knees, and she had her right arm in a sling. The arm that the sling supported was in plaster.

Miss Sharples had come into the room behind Charlotte.

"There now, isn't this nice?" Miss Sharples said. "Miss Cambrey has come to see you. And this is Nurse Wallace, Miss Cambrey, who came to look after Mrs. Frensham when she was taken ill."

"Taken ill, taken ill!" the old woman exclaimed, her prune-dark eyes swivelling to look up at Charlotte without moving her head. "Why can't you say when I had my bloody stroke? Are you afraid of the word, stroke? That's what I had, and it's a wonder that I can think or move at all. But I've always had a remarkable constitution. All the same, the next one I have, I shall die. And this silly woman will say then that I've passed on, or gone to my rest, or something equally ridiculous, because she's afraid of the word death. She can never bring herself to say that my stepson's dead. Dead! Dead! That's what he is, but the idiot can't say it. Well, Emily, what are you standing there for? Why can't you bring us our coffee? Three cups it had better be. Get a move on!"

Miss Sharples gave Charlotte a little smile and withdrew, closing the door softly behind her.

"Well, sit down, for God's sake!" Mrs. Frensham snapped at Charlotte. "I don't like having to strain my neck, looking up at you. You've come for a reason, I suppose. You don't just want to stand there, staring at me like some bloody reporter. We've had enough of those. Say what you want to say, then leave us in peace."

Charlotte sat down in one of the flowery chairs and was just going to speak when the big woman gave her a sudden, wide smile and said, "You're the young lady who's living in Beech Cottage, aren't you? That was my own dear little home till I went away."

"I'm only staying there for a short time," Charlotte said.
"I took it for a month, but I don't expect I shall stay as long
as that."

"Just you wait and see," Mrs. Frensham said. "You don't
know how long the police will keep you here. They've been
asking me a lot of questions about you, d'you know that?"

"I expect that was because of my brother," Charlotte
said. "Did they ask you why Mr. Frensham let the cottage
to someone called Cambrey?"

The fierce old eyes considered her shrewdly.

"Yes, that's just what they asked. What could I tell them?
I didn't interfere with the way Edgar ran the estate. It was
good for him to have some responsibility."

"But you know he was a witness against my brother
recently when he was tried for robbing a bank."

Nurse Wallace caught her breath with a little hissing
sound.

Mrs. Frensham made a gesture with one of her arthritic
hands as if she were brushing away something of no importance.

"Oh, that—yes," she said. "Nothing to do with me. I don't
know anything about it. Is that what you came to talk to me
about?"

"No, I really wanted to ask you about a man called
Royle."

Nurse Wallace gave a little cough. "If I may interrupt for
a moment, if that cottage is really going to be available
soon, dear Mrs. Frensham, you'll give me the first refusal of
it, won't you? I'd be so happy to live there again, and I
could always pop up here to help you any time you needed
it." She turned to Charlotte. "I only gave the cottage up because I had the wonderful opportunity of spending the winter in Madeira with a lovely old couple who needed nursing
care. But then, when we'd only been there three weeks, I

slipped on some steps and broke my wrist. It's nothing serious and it's coming along nicely, but of course I couldn't be any use to the old people, so I came home. And I'd like so much to settle into that cottage again. I'm sure Mr. Frensham would have wanted me to have it."

"He couldn't have cared less, so long as he got the rent," Mrs. Frensham said. "What's this about that man Royle?"

"He's a detective," Charlotte said, "and I wanted to know if you employed him."

"Of course I did, though I don't see what business it is of yours," the old woman said impatiently. "But I sacked him yesterday. What was the point of paying him when he'd turned out bloody useless? I wanted him to find out for me discreetly what Edgar was up to, installing a safe, which was ridiculous if all the money he was handling was what the estate brought in. Then I happened to hear of those people Hargreave's from a friend, who said they were very efficient and very discreet, and I asked them to send a man down to look into matters for me. And all he's told me is what the police have told me too."

"I suppose when Mr. Royle took the job on he didn't know there was going to be a murder, with police all over the place," Charlotte said. "If things hadn't happened like that, he might have been quite useful."

"One doesn't pay people on the basis of what they might have done if things had been different," Mrs. Frensham replied. "One pays for results. And it was the police, not Royle, who told me there were documents in the safe that showed my dear stepson had been running a nice little line in black mail. He'd got evidence that an unfortunate man in Mattingley called Entwistle had been taking bribes, and when the man heard the police had got the safe open, the foolish creature committed suicide. And there were things Edgar was holding over other people too, among them—

would you believe it?—my dear Ralph Maynard. Edgar'd made some notes on the number of elderly patients of Ralph's who'd died a bit suddenly, leaving him legacies, and I think he was getting ready to squeeze Ralph dry. But did Royle find out any of this? No, I got it all from Superintendent Barr, who told me about it because he wanted to know if I'd left Ralph anything in my will."

"And have you?" Charlotte asked. She remembered how anxious Dr. Maynard had been to discover what was in the safe.

"Certainly," the old woman said. "We have an arrangement. If I get so paralyzed I'm helpless, or if my mind begins to go, he's going to give me a nice shot of morphine one night and I'm not going to wake up. And on that understanding, I've left him five hundred pounds. I thought about the sum very carefully. It's not big enough to be a temptation, but it'll be a nice present to be given suddenly. I think it's just about the right amount."

"Now, dear Mrs. Frensham," Nurse Wallace said, looking a little pale, "you know that's a very naughty way to talk. I know it's only a joke, but perhaps Miss Cambrey, who doesn't know you as well as I do, won't understand that, and she might repeat it and it might do harm. Dr. Maynard would never come to an arrangement like that with anyone."

"Oh, oh, wouldn't he just!" Mrs. Frensham gave a little crow of laughter. "Why else did Mrs. Meadows leave him that fine Jaguar he runs if she wasn't promised that she'd have a nice easy end? And all those fine wines he inherited from Colonel James, who died soon after he'd made his will —why were they left to Ralph? The colonel died quietly and peacefully after years of pain. I'm sure he was very grateful."

"But you're accusing Dr. Maynard of murder!" Nurse

Wallace moaned. "A fine man like Dr. Maynard! You mustn't say such things."

"Don't be a bloody fool. Of course I'm accusing him of murder." The old woman was enjoying herself. Her great, dark eyes became almost young-looking with the sparkle of malice. "Lots of doctors go in for a bit of murder on the side, you know that as well as I do. I shouldn't be surprised if you've helped them sometimes. And Ralph's a good, kind man who hates seeing people suffer, and I'm sure there are lots of people he's quietly finished off without getting a penny for it. And that's all right for poor people, but I don't think it's fair when one can afford to recompense him for taking a risk. I only hope Edgar hadn't collected enough evidence for the police to be able to bring a prosecution." She turned suddenly to Charlotte. "Well?" she barked at her. "What are you waiting for? You wanted to know if I employed Royle. Yes, I did, and then I sacked him. Is he complaining about that?"

"No," Charlotte said.

"Is he a friend of yours?"

"I think he is, in a way," she answered hesitantly. "But there's something else I'd like to ask . . ."

As she hesitated the old woman snapped at her, "Get on with it. I'm feeling very tired."

"Was there any money in the safe?"

"None at all."

"Do you know where Mr. Frensham kept his money?"

"He didn't keep it, he spent it."

"But hadn't he any money of his own? What you say he was making from black mail, for instance, where did he put that?"

"He'd a bank account in Mattingley, but the police told me there's very little in it. But he'd a lot of extravagant tastes. I shouldn't think he ever saved a penny." A kind of film seemed to come over the glinting old eyes, then the eye-lids drooped over them. Mrs. Frensham leant her head back against the cushions in her chair. In a feeble voice, quite unlike the one that she had been using, she murmured, "I'm very tired. I'd like to go and lie down. Nurse, will you help me up? And tell Emily I'll have my coffee in bed. You can have yours with this child. Only be careful what you say to her. She wants to know too bloody much."

Almost visibly she seemed to shrink in her chair, becoming pathetic and helpless.

Nurse Wallace stood up, clicking her tongue disapprovingly.

"It's all been too much for her," she said. "She's got over-excited. You shouldn't have asked her such a lot of questions. But the young never understand the needs of the old. They show no consideration. If I were you, I'd go home before I did any more damage."

"I'm going," Charlotte said. "I've found out several things I wanted to know."

"I shouldn't take them too seriously," Nurse Wallace said. "She's always had a love of making mischief. The things she said about Dr. Maynard—good gracious me!"

"Suppose they're true," Charlotte said.

At that moment she noticed that one of Mrs. Frensham's eyes was open, peering at her, but it fluttered shut as soon as she saw that Charlotte had seen it. Charlotte let herself out of the room and crossed the hall to the front door.

She was just putting her hand on the latch when Miss Sharples appeared in the hall, carrying a tray with three cups and a pot of coffee on it.

"Oh, aren't you staying for your coffee, dear?" she asked. "Mrs. Frensham will be so disappointed. She loves company."

"I think she's had enough of mine," Charlotte answered.

"You've been talking about Mr. Edgar, I expect," Miss Sharples said. "Naturally that's upset her. Poor woman, she really did her best for him, as if he was her own son. She didn't let even me know the truth about him. I can hardly believe it even now I've heard it all from the police. You've heard that story about his farming in South Africa, I expect. Well, there wasn't a word of truth in it. Actually he'd been in prison for three years before he came here. Some sort of fraud, I think it was. And he'd been in trouble before that too, something to do with faking antiques. He was using a false name to do that, of course, but the police know all about it now. They got it from his finger-prints. That's so clever of them, isn't it? And everyone will know all about it soon, and that'll hurt her, you know. It may even kill her. She brought him here after the last time he came out of gaol to see if she could keep him out of any more trouble, and she let him handle all her affairs to show she trusted him. She loved his father very much, you see, and she's very good and kind in her way. You're sure you won't stay for coffee? Oh well, good-bye for now, dear."

CHAPTER EIGHT

Charlotte was about half-way down the drive, on her way back to the Graingers' cottage, when she realized that she had forgotten to take the key which Mrs. Grainger had told her she would leave on the kitchen table. So, when Charlotte reached the cottage, she naturally found herself locked out. The only thing to do, in the circumstances, was to return to Beech Cottage.

Not that she was unwilling to do this. She had lost the feeling that she had had about it the evening before and would have been ready to settle into it again if she had been able to recover her belongings from the other cottage. However, she would be able to do that later in the day, when the Graingers returned from Mattingley. She walked the short distance along the main road to Beech Cottage and pushed open the squeaking gate.

She found Timothy Royle sitting in the porch, where she had found him the day before. He stood up as she walked up the path. His sharp features were pinched by the cold and he looked as if he had not slept much.

"I've been wondering where you'd got to," he said. "Seeing the curtains drawn and all, I was beginning to worry that something was wrong, and I was beginning to consider breaking in to see if you were all right."

"How would you have gone about that?" she asked. "Broken a window?"

"If I'd had to, but I've got keys that will cope with most things."

"Well, I just took your advice," she said. "I went to see Mrs. Frensham. So now I know you aren't employed by her any more, though you were when you came down here. I think it was splitting hairs yesterday to say you weren't working for her."

"Splitting hairs isn't a bad basis for honesty," he said. "If it turned out she didn't want you to know I'd worked for her at all, I shouldn't have said anything about it."

She took her key out of her handbag and opened the cottage door. The room inside felt very cold and the jasmine in the vase on the table had shed its flowers. They lay scattered round the vase on the imitation rosewood, shrivelled and brown. It seemed to her that there was a mustiness about the place as if it had stood empty for more than a single night.

As she took off her jacket, she said, "I spent last night at the Graingers'. After what happened here I felt, oh, sort of exposed, as if anyone who felt like it could walk in. And they'd asked me to stay with them if I wanted to." She switched on the electric fire and drew back the crimson curtains, letting cold, grey light into the room. "I think I'll make some coffee."

"That sounds like a good idea."

She went to the kitchen, plugged in the kettle, then put her head back into the living-room.

"Why did you come here this morning?" she asked. "Your job's finished, isn't it?"

He had taken off his overcoat and sat down with his hands held out to the bars of the fire, which were beginning to glow.

"It'll only be finished when I'm satisfied with the conclusion," he said.

"But nobody's paying you, so why don't you go home? There may be another job waiting for you there."

"I think someone may pay me here before I'm through."

"You aren't thinking of me, are you, because I couldn't possibly afford to hire a detective all to myself, however badly I might need him."

"I have been thinking of you, as a matter of fact, though not as a source of income. More as a source of information and also as someone who may get herself in a hell of a mess if someone doesn't look after her."

"That sounds like the paternal streak in you coming out," she said. "But I'm not worried about myself any more. Yesterday I was. I had a fit of panic." The kettle had begun to steam. She turned back into the kitchen, put some generous spoonfuls of coffee into a jug, poured boiling water over them and left it to stand while she put cups and saucers, milk and a strainer on a tray. Then when she thought the coffee was ready, she carried the tray into the sitting-room. "Have you heard how things have gone with Mrs. Neville?"

He gave an enormous yawn before he answered, then leant back, folding his hands behind his head and looking as if he might fall asleep in another minute.

"I spent most of the night in the hospital," he said. "She's holding her own, but only just. I don't think they're too hopeful. The bullet missed her heart, but went into her left lung. And I got it from Barr, after they'd dug it out, that it looks very much as if it came from the same gun that killed Frensham. But they haven't really had time to make sure. It seems obvious, of course, that it should have come from the same gun, but there's always the chance that we've two separate murderers around. However, one thing we can be fairly sure of now, whatever she was doing up at Brickett's Farm when you saw her there, is that she didn't kill Frensham. That coffee smells awfully good."

"I told you I went to Brickett's this morning," Charlotte said as she poured it into the two cups. "I had a few minutes talk with Miss Sharples and she was just bubbling over with some information she'd got hold of. She said Frensham had never been to South Africa, as he'd told everyone, but had been in and out of prison most of his life till Mrs. Frensham got him here to try to reform him. Miss Sharples said the police found out about it all from his finger-prints. So I was right all along, wasn't I, and he was a crook and the evidence he gave against Dick didn't mean a thing? Dick was just the victim he chose to have a fight with so that the others who were working with him could get away with the money. Dick had nothing to do with it . . ." Her calm voice abruptly choked. She nearly dropped the cup of coffee that she was handing to Royle, then, as he took it from her, she sank into a chair, covered her face with her hands and to her own surprise, began crying with shattering sobs. It felt as if something frozen inside her had suddenly melted, letting the tears come streaming out of her in a strong, healing flood.

Royle sipped a little coffee, stood up and sat down on the arm of her chair. He put an arm round her shoulders and drew her against him.

"That's why you really came to Mattingley, isn't it?" he said. "Because you weren't sure. You hoped you could find out the truth from Frensham, and now you have, though I don't think you would have if he'd been alive. If Frensham organized that robbery, and we can be fairly sure he did, then your brother's innocent."

She leant her head against him, feeling him gently stroking her shoulder.

"But there was the woman in the bank who recognized him," she said, beginning to control her sobbing. "I'm sure she was quite honest and believed what she said."

"Identification of that sort is always pretty dubious," he said. "That's recognized now. The evidence of someone in a state of terror isn't at all reliable. She'd seen your brother come in after the other two men, and when Frensham said they'd come in together she was sure he was right. Now drink your coffee and cheer up. This can be sorted out."

She drew away from him, mopping at her eyes with her handkerchief, then reached for her cup.

"You can be very nice, you know," she said. "Very comforting. But what do I do next?"

"We talk to Barr," he said. "I told you I thought he was a fair man. He may have arrived at the same conclusions as you already. Then you talk to your solicitor. Have you a good solicitor?"

"Not very," she said. "At least, he never did much to help Dick."

"I know a very good one," he said. "You need to in my job. You can go to him, and he can take over before Dick's case comes up for appeal. We'll get him out, you'll see. But why have you been so frightened that he might be guilty? I know you said he couldn't be, but it seemed to me there was a lot of fear behind it."

The coffee was steadying her. She drew a deep breath.

"He was always such a crazy boy," she said. "What I told you was quite true, the only time he got into trouble with the police was when he went joy-riding in a neighbour's car and got bound over. But there'd been other things I knew about. . . . He had a phase of shop-lifting when he was about fourteen. It was just a kind of sport to him, he didn't really want the things he stole, and he grew out of it. Then when he was about eighteen he had a very unhappy love-affair and went on to marijuana, but that didn't last long either. He'd rather a habit of having unhappy love-affairs, but he swore to me he'd never go back to drugs, and I don't think he did. But he couldn't keep jobs. Sometimes within a few days of starting a new one, he'd quarrel with his boss and get fired. I think that's why the girl he was living with when he was arrested went straight off and married someone else. She wanted a home and a steady income and children, and she didn't see Dick ever giving them to her. But he told me he understood it perfectly and that he knew he was no use to her and didn't bear her any malice. He's such a gentle person, I couldn't imagine him doing anything violent. And he swore to me he'd had nothing to do with the robbery. He said he hadn't even the faintest idea how you'd start robbing a bank, even if you wanted to. And I was sure he was speaking the truth, but at the same time . . . at the same time, you see . . ." Her voice choked again and she could feel the tears starting.

"Yes, I see," Royle said. "He's been quite a problem for you, hasn't he? Quite a heavy responsibility for someone of your age. I don't wonder you've had your doubts. But I'll tell you what we're going to do now. We're going into Mattingley and we're going to have the best lunch we can get. I warn you, that isn't going to be anything very special. Mattingley isn't very well off for restaurants, but it'll do you good. It'll do me good too. I get tired of eating alone. We'll go to the White Horse. That's where I'm staying and it isn't too bad. And you can tell me something I'm curious about. Did your brother ever give you any description of the two men who came into the bank and got away with the money?"

"Oh yes," she said. "He said they were both dressed in blue jeans and black leather jackets and had rather long brown hair and bushy dark beards and dark glasses. And one had a gun and the other a bag that he stuffed the money into."

"Were they tall or short?"

"About medium, I think."

"Thin, bony, heavily built or what?"

"I don't think he mentioned that, but I think about average."

"And they'd no nylon stockings over their heads, or any other kind of mask?"

She shook her head. "I don't think so."

"Then we can be fairly sure the beards and perhaps the long hair too were false and could be peeled off as soon as they got away from the bank. They vanished successfully, anyway. Yet Frensham must have been in touch with them. Perhaps if the police are convinced of that now, they'll be able to trace a connection. Now let's go." He looked at his watch. "There's a bus due in a few minutes. Just mop your face up a bit and you'll soon feel better."

Charlotte went upstairs, washed her face, thought that she would put on a little make-up, then wondered if they would miss the bus if she lingered to do it, combed her hair quickly, went downstairs again, put on her jacket and, remembering to switch off the fire, opened the door, and she and Royle went out into the garden.

A light rain had started since she had come back from Brickett's Farm. It was hardly more than a mist, but its chill on her face was a curiously pleasant sensation, making her feel that it would soon wash away what was left of her tear-stains. The Mattingley bus came by only a minute or two later and she and Royle climbed on board. It was a single-decker bus, not very full. Because it was half-empty the conversations going on inside it were all audible, and except for one, between two solidly built village women whose minds were firmly anchored to the price of beef, they were all about murder. Murder past and present, local and far away. Everyone seemed to have some knowledge of it, even if it was only at second or third hand. Murder in general was in some way far more urgent to discuss than the one that had happened on their own door-steps. When that was mentioned an uneasy silence fell. There was the sense in it of a horror that had come a little too close to be borne. Charlotte looked out at the dripping hedges, more conscious than she had expected of the nearness of the thin man beside her and not sure if she was more disturbed or comforted by it.

The bus terminal in Mattingley was opposite the railway station. There was a large, crowded car-park between them. The White Horse Hotel also faced the station. It was a Victorian building, rather forbidding, painted grey, with its tall windows shrouded in net and with a pillared porch sheltering a few steps that led up to an open door.

Inside there was a narrow hall, carpeted in a startling pattern of maroon and yellow, with hunting prints on the walls and a pervasive smell of boiled mutton. Royle guided Charlotte into a small bar where the same colourful carpet glared up at them from the floor and several small round tables with copper tops stood here and there with chairs surrounding them, covered in cold, shiny leatherette. There was no one sitting at any of the tables, but there were two men sitting on stools at the bar, eating sandwiches and drinking what looked like vodka. They were Ian Havershaw and Marcus Neville.

They did not look round at once when the door opened and Charlotte and Royle entered the room, but with their elbows on the bar and their heads close together, appeared to be in some intimate discussion. It was Ian Havershaw who looked round first when Royle went up to the bar and ordered drinks. Charlotte had settled herself at one of the small tables. Ian's fair hair was disordered, as if it had been raked in all directions by his fingers, and his freckles stood out like spots on a plover's egg on a face that had become

much paler than when she had seen it last. The smile that
appeared on it, showing his large, uneven teeth, looked uneasy and forced.

"Hallo," he said. "You haven't any news, I suppose."

"About Mrs. Neville?" Royle turned to the barman who
had appeared through a door behind the bar and ordered
two whiskies.

"Yes, yes, of course, Isobel," Marcus Neville said. If he
had been up most of the night, waiting for news of his wife,
he did not show it. His thick, auburn hair was smooth. He
had shaved recently. His red-velvet suit looked spruce and
well-brushed. Only the shadows under his greenish eyes
suggested that, in fact, he had not slept much.

"I haven't been in the hospital for the last hour or so,"
Royle said. "When I left they said there was still a chance
for her."

"That's what they told us," Ian Havershaw said. "Of
course, they wouldn't let us in to see her, not even to look at
her from the door. There was a policeman there in the cor-
ridor and as soon as she can talk they'll let him in to question her, which I find inhuman. They ought to think of
whom she'd want to see when she recovers consciousness
and that isn't going to be some dough-faced copper she's
never seen before. It'll probably frighten her. They ought to
let us in."

"Both of you?" Royle asked, paying for the drinks and
carrying them across to the table where Charlotte was sitting.

"Oh, I don't expect they'd let both of us in together,"
Neville said, biting into a sandwich. "It might excite her,
having too many people round her. But I don't see why they
shouldn't let us in one at a time."

"Which of you first?" Royle asked as he sat down.

"It doesn't matter," Havershaw said. "Marcus can go

first, if he likes. I just don't think she should open her eyes
and find herself looking at a dough-faced copper. She
should see a familiar face, a loving face." He turned to
Neville and put a hand on his shoulder. "Don't you think
I'm right, Marcus? That's what she needs, a loving face, full
of tenderness and concern."

"That's right," Neville said, nodding his head several
times. "Do you know, I like you, Ian. You've a lot of understanding."

It had dawned on Charlotte that both men were fairly
drunk.

"You can go first, if you want to, Marcus," Havershaw
said. "I like you too. I want you to do just whatever you
like."

"No, you go first," Neville said. "We've got to think what
would be best for Isobel. So you go first. That's what she'd
like."

"Oh, I don't know that she would," Havershaw replied.
"She's still very fond of you, you know. She's always told
me what a high regard she has for you. A brilliant man,
she's always said, who'll astonish everyone some day. She
likes brilliant men, have you noticed that? She always said
to me I was brilliant and that I'd astonish everyone some
day."

"And I'm sure you will," Neville said, his head going on
nodding as if he had lost the mechanism that would stop it.
"She's been very lucky really, knowing so many brilliant
men. Only Frensham wasn't brilliant. Have you ever
thought about that? He hadn't a grain of intellect. He was a
crude, dull, thick-headed bore. Yet she fell in love with him.
Extraordinary, really. Not her type at all."

"She was never in love with him," Havershaw said, finishing his vodka and thrusting out his glass for a refill. "Infatuated, yes, but let me tell you that's a very different thing

from being in love. I know a lot about that. It happens to me very easily. But it doesn't mean anything." He thrust his face close to Neville's. "Are you listening to me? I don't think you are. I said she'd never been in love with Frensham."

"She's never been in love with anyone but me," Neville said, his voice suddenly full of a deep sadness. He appeared not to have noticed the aggressive note that had sounded in Ian Havershaw's. "That's what's so unbearable, to know that and not to be able to get her to understand it. Sometimes I've wondered if she isn't really a stupid woman. If she is, that would explain a lot. But I don't know. I know she's unbalanced and hysterical, but I've never been able to make up my mind if she's stupid. I have a great contempt for stupid people, do you know that? Thou shalt not suffer a fool to live—in my opinion that ought to be one of the commandments."

"No, no, you're quite wrong," Havershaw said with growing excitement. "That's intolerant. People can't help being fools. I don't believe they can help being wicked either, but one has to draw the line somewhere. But one mustn't be intolerant. You aren't really intolerant, are you, Marcus? You're kind and understanding, just like me. She always said so, except sometimes, when she was angry with you. She said she knew you would understand about her and me, how much we love one another. Not an infatuation this time. Absolutely not."

Neville suddenly began pounding the counter in front of him with a clenched fist.

"I do not understand it!" he shouted. "I do not believe it! If she loved you so much, why didn't she go to you last night instead of Miss Cambrey? Can you tell me that?"

"How can I tell you when I don't know what she came

for? And when I don't know why she went away. I don't know that any more than you do."

"Well, I can tell you why she didn't go to you." Neville's face reddened deeply with the unpredictable anger of the drunk. "It's simple as hell. She didn't go to you because she didn't want to see you. You're a fool if you can't see that. And if she didn't want to see you, it's because she isn't in love with you. That's logical, isn't it? Simple as hell. You're a terrible fool, my dear Ian, if you think that woman's been in love with you for a minute. But you can go in to see her first, if you want to. That's because you're younger than me. The young are privileged. They get first turns at everything. I can't think why they should, but it's a fact in our society, and I am not an anarchist. I accept the rules of society."

Royle stood up. He and Charlotte had finished their drinks.

"The first person to see her will be that dough-faced policeman," he said, "and after that it's anybody's guess. She may have some ideas of her own." He looked at Charlotte. "Shall we go and see what they've got for lunch?"

She stood up too. But just as she turned to the door it opened and Dr. Maynard came in. At first, as if he had not seen that there was anyone else in the room, he went straight to the bar and ordered a whisky. His plump face looked drawn and revealingly tired. But as soon as he had taken in who else was in the bar with him, he managed to rearrange his features into their professional blandness and even produced a smile.

"Good news," he said. "Splendid. You'll all be glad to hear it. Mrs. Neville's doing fine. Sleeping now, but definitely on the way to recovery. I've just come from the hospital, and I can assure you there's nothing to worry about."

The words had an instantly sobering effect on Marcus

Neville and Ian Havershaw. They drew apart from one another, neither friends nor enemies any more.

"You're sure of this?" Neville said. "There's no mistake?"

"She's really out of danger?" Havershaw said.

"Well, short of the Almighty taking it out of the hands of mere doctors, which can always happen," Dr. Maynard said, "I think you can rest assured."

"I suppose," Royle said, "she hasn't done any talking yet."

"No, I don't know when she'll be fit for that."

Royle took Charlotte by the arm and urged her towards the door.

"Perhaps, when it comes to the point, she'll prefer not to do any talking at all," he said.

They went out together and made their way along a murky passage to the dining-room.

It was a big room with a few people already at lunch in it. The ceiling was high, the windows, which looked towards the railway station, were long and shrouded in net, the tables had small vases of plastic flowers on each. The smell of boiled mutton was even stronger here than in the passage, mingled with the smell of stale coffee.

An elderly waitress took them to a table in front of one of the windows. Charlotte liked the feeling of being at a window until she became aware of the draught that came in bitingly from round the ill-fitting old window-frames. If she had known Timothy Royle better she might have suggested moving, but she did not want him to take her for one of the women who cannot go into a restaurant without protesting at something or other, determined at all costs to draw attention to themselves. Sitting down, she merely kept her jacket draped over her shoulders and began to study the menu that the waitress handed to her before she noticed that the Graingers were at the table in front of the neighbouring window and trying to attract her attention by waving their paper napkins at her. They had just paid their bill and were preparing to leave.

"How are you?" Mrs. Grainger called out. "Did you find the key in the kitchen? I'm sorry we had to go out, but as I told you, we had an appointment with our lawyer, and I'm glad to say everything's been signed up now, so we'll be able to leave Rose Cottage and move into our flat in a day or two. We're meeting the architect there this afternoon to discuss the alterations we want made. We'd meant to stay at the cottage until the work was done, instead of living in the middle of the awful mess they'll make, but the truth is, we don't care for living at Brickett's any more. Ben says it's silly of me, but I really don't like the feeling of the place now. I suppose you've no news of poor Mrs. Neville."

"As a matter of fact, Dr. Maynard came into the bar a few minutes ago," Charlotte said, "and he says she's doing splendidly. He says she's asleep now, but quite out of danger."

"Well, isn't that wonderful!" Mrs. Neville exclaimed. She turned to her husband. "Ben, isn't that wonderful? Actually I had a sort of feeling all along that she'd pull through. I'm like that, you know. I have these sort of intuitions that I can't explain, but I usually trust them. You'd be surprised how often I'm right. Ben, isn't that true? Aren't I right nine times out of ten?"

"I've never kept count," he answered drily. He stood up, pocketing the change that the waitress had brought. "She'll be staying in the hospital for the present, I imagine, but I wonder where she'll go when they let her out. She lives all alone and they generally turn you out before you're fit to look after yourself."

"Well, I know at least two men who'd very gladly look after her," Mrs. Grainger said coyly. "And there's always

Nurse Wallace. I believe she's staying in this hotel. She could help, even if she's only got the use of one arm. I think I'll look for her and ask her if she's free, then I'll visit Mrs. Neville and tell her it's all fixed up. It'll be a weight off her mind."

"I don't think they're letting anyone visit her yet," Royle said.

"And anyway, it isn't our business," Mr. Grainger said.

"But it is," his wife insisted. "She's a friend of ours, isn't she? Well, at least a neighbour. And she's in trouble. People are always saying things aren't their business when they could easily give some help. I'm not like that. I'll make a point of talking to Nurse Wallace."

She buttoned up her jacket, tied a scarf over her hair and she and her husband went out.

The waitress had come to Charlotte and Royle's table, and they both ordered vegetable soup and roast sirloin. The soup, they found, had certainly come out of a packet, but it was warming.

"I wonder," Royle observed after a brief silence, "if Dr. Maynard's good news was really good news to everyone who heard it."

Charlotte wrinkled her forehead. "Are you suspicious of one of us?"

"Not of anyone in particular," he said. "But someone will be very sorry that that shot didn't kill Mrs. Neville and that she's going to be able to talk. And it may be one of the people we've been talking to this morning."

"I suppose that has to be the reason why she was shot," Charlotte said. "To stop her talking about whatever she saw at Brickett's Farm. Do you think she actually saw the murder?"

"It doesn't seem unlikely."

"But how did he know she was coming to see me last night? I didn't know it myself."

"Anyone who recognized her white Renault in the road outside your gate might have shot her."

Their soup-plates were removed and were replaced by plates on which limp slices of sirloin swam in glutinous brown gravy.

"Oh hell!" Royle muttered as he attacked his. "This is awful. Worse than I feared. I wanted to take you out to a good lunch. You looked as if you needed it." He seemed really put out.

"It doesn't matter," Charlotte said. "I'm quite happy."

"You must come out to lunch with me one day in London and have a really decent meal when all this mess is over," he said.

"Will you bring all five children with you?" she asked. "Not to mention your wife. I'd like to meet them, but it'll come awfully expensive."

He shot her a doubtful glance. "As it happens, my wife isn't at all jealous or interfering. I often take female clients out to lunch. She has no objections."

"I'm not a client."

"That's just a technicality. You're helping me with a case."

"But you're off the case."

"As I told you, I'm off a job when I take myself off it."

"I wonder what really makes you tick," she said.

"I don't like to feel defeated."

"Is that how you feel now?"

"Yes and no."

"That means you've some ideas about the case, but you aren't sure of them."

"Not sure at all. I keep thinking about the woman who

wrote the letters in the safe. You're sure they couldn't have been written by Isobel Neville?"·

"I saw that receipt she wrote for me and the letter Mr. Barr let me have a glimpse of. There was absolutely no resemblance in the handwriting."

"So we've got to find someone else. And perhaps we'll never do that. It could be someone who's never even been near here. There's just one thing against that. Someone here hated or feared Isobel Neville so much that she tried to murder her."

"You're saying 'she' now," Charlotte said. "Do you think it was a woman who murdered Edgar Frensham?"

"Why not?" He abandoned some stringy remains of his beef. "Look, I'm really sorry about this. We'd have done better having sandwiches in the bar."

She laughed. "In spite of murder, one must eat, you think," she said. "One must keep one's strength up. I suppose it's important to remember that in your kind of job."

"I believe in trying to go on living as normally as possible even through the worst crisis," he answered. "One should always do one's best to hold on to every-day things. Look how people managed in the war. My parents told me how they used to go to theatres and concerts and visit their friends and ask them back to dinner with omelets made of powdered egg, even when the bombs were falling."

"I should think the powdered egg must have been the hardest thing to face."

He gave her a worried look. "You know, there are times when I don't think you take me quite seriously."

"Am I meant to?"

"Oh God, the child is altogether too shrewd," he said. "You look so young, but you talk like an adult. It's very hard to know what to make of you. And you've actually finished that beef. That's a sign of healthy youth, if ever I saw one."

"It's no worse than my own cooking," she said.

"Well, would you like some rhubarb pie and custard now?" he asked.

"Yes, please."

"Then you can eat that by yourself, because it's something I won't face. I'll just sit and watch you, which is something I don't mind doing in any case."

"I'm glad you brought me here," she assured him. "If you hadn't, we shouldn't have heard that fascinating talk in the bar. I wonder what those two men really feel about one another."

"A good, old-fashioned hatred," he said. "But that reminds me, if you don't mind going home on the bus on your own, I'll go back to the hospital and ask how Mrs. Neville is coming along. And perhaps I'll be able to find out if anyone else has been asking after her. That might be interesting."

"The murderer will ask after her, is that what you think?"

"Probably, among others."

All at once she did not want her rhubarb pie and custard at all. She did not want coffee either. She only wanted suddenly and very much to be at home in her flat in Maida Vale, sorting through notes made for her by her old general, trying to put them into some sort of order, wrapped in blessed dullness, without a thought of murder in her mind.

But the general was dead and Dick was in prison and she had taken up a task which she felt she could not lay down. Perhaps that was a little how Timothy Royle was feeling at the moment. But she became listless, brooding on the woman in the hospital, wondering if the truth was that she was in some danger, and when Royle tried to go on talking, she hardly responded. Presently they left the restaurant and she went to the bus stop outside the station.

The light, almost mist-like rain was still falling. Standing in the bus queue she felt very cold. She asked the woman standing next to her when the next bus to the village was due and was told that she had ten minutes to wait. In ten minutes, she thought, as she turned up the collar of her coat, she could become very wet. If the rain was not heavy, it was penetrating. She did not pay any attention to the car that had just been driven out of the car-park beside the station and stopped in front of the queue until the woman next to her dug her in the ribs and said, "I think it's you he wants."

Charlotte started and realized that the driver of the car, who was trying to attract her attention, was Ian Havershaw.

"Want a lift home?" he asked, leaning out. He sounded as if he had sobered up since he had seen her last.

"Oh, thank you, yes." Gratefully she scrambled into the car. "This is marvellous luck for me. It's freezing cold, standing there in the rain."

"It's luck for me too," he said as he started the car again. "As a matter of fact, I want to talk to you."

CHAPTER NINE

Whatever Ian Havershaw wanted to talk to Charlotte about, it appeared at first not to be murder and to begin with he drove in silence. Then after a little he said, "I wasn't really as drunk as I expect I sounded. I'm sorry you heard it at all. It was just that the general strain of things was making me light-headed. I've been going nearly crazy with worry."

"Well, you can stop worrying now," Charlotte said. "Mrs. Neville's going to recover."

"That's only one of the things I've been worrying about," he said. "I still don't know where she vanished to, or why, and I think Marcus does, or why did he come here in the first place? Well, never mind about that now. I left it to him to go and see her in visiting hours this afternoon, if they're letting anyone in at all, and I'm going to meet him again later on to hear how things are. I hated letting him be the one to go in, but we thought they were more likely to let her husband in than someone like me. You know, I'd find things much easier if I could honestly dislike him, but I can't—and I think he feels the same about me. If it weren't for Isobel, I think we'd be good friends."

"As a writer, isn't that just the kind of thing you've got to try to understand?" Charlotte said.

"You're absolutely right," he answered gravely. "But it would be much easier to understand if it was happening to someone else and not myself."

"Doesn't your understanding of other people come out of understanding of yourself?" she asked.

"Oh yes, absolutely." He lapsed into silence again. Presently he continued, "Of course, you don't take this thing seriously about me trying to be a writer."

"I don't see why not," she said.

"Don't you think I'm too young? Don't you think there's something rather ridiculous about it?"

"I suppose, if you want to do it at all, you've got to start some time or other."

"But perhaps one ought to do rather more living first."

"I'd have said you'd been doing quite a lot of it lately."

He gave her a quick glance and smiled his oddly attractive, toothy smile.

"I do like you," he said. "Talking to you really does me good. And what I suddenly thought of talking to you about when I saw you standing there was—well, of course say no if you don't like the idea, but I was going to ask you, if you aren't fearfully busy with something else just now, whether you'd care to look at my manuscript. I'm absolutely stuck at the moment, and I thought if I could talk it over with someone else, it'd help. In the ordinary way, I'd talk it over with Isobel, but I don't know how long it's going to be before I can do that, and if I could only get working again now, it'd help to pass the time." He smiled again, but his tone was earnest. "You probably think I'm a fantastic egotist."

It was just what Charlotte had been thinking, but his saying so himself disarmed her. She guessed that he had a great need to talk of something, anything, that was not murder.

"I'd love to see your manuscript," she said, though the thought dismayed her. She did not feel in the least like reading. She felt far too restless and confused. But who knew, perhaps he was a genius and in years to come she would be able to claim that she had been among the first people to recognize his talent. She would not be able to claim that she had discovered him, since Isobel Neville had been before her, but at least she would be able to say that she had encouraged him, guided him and helped him through a crisis in his life when he had felt himself close to defeat. She rather liked to think of herself in this role, even if she did not take it very seriously.

But unfortunately, when she settled down a little later in her own cottage to read his novel, she saw no signs of genius. He had driven her down the weedy drive to his cottage, the converted barn that she had seen next to Isobel Neville's, had taken her in, opened a cupboard and brought out a file in which there was a neat pile of typescript. It had surprised Charlotte a little to discover that he was a very neat person. The room into which he had taken her, and which was furnished in much the same way as her own living-room, had none of the litter of papers and books or the dust and even the cobwebs that she had expected. A typewriter with a cover on it stood on the table. There was a box of typing paper beside it and also a book that she took to be a dictionary. He appeared to be a good housekeeper.

But he was not a very good writer. She could not deceive herself about that when she had read a chapter. However, she recognized that she was not exactly a competent literary critic. Perhaps the work was far more promising than it seemed to her. Perhaps someone with better judgement would be able to see this. But there was something very juvenile about it, something that seemed even more immature than Ian himself. Charlotte sensed this in spite of her own immaturity. And she noticed a curious thing about the typescript. The seventy pages or so of it were surprisingly yellow, as if they had been lying in his cupboard for some time. She began to wonder if his desire to be a writer had ever been anything but a daydream from which he might have roused himself long ago if he had not happened to fall in love with Isobel Neville, who had well-meaningly but mistakenly encouraged him. Charlotte also wondered if getting stuck, as he had told her he was, had not been a matter of a few days, or at most a week or two, but months or more. In any case, she thought, the sooner he gave it up and went back to making a lot of money teaching in Saudi Arabia, the better.

But she struggled on to the end of the seventy pages, then wondering what she could say to him that would be neither too hurtful nor too flagrantly dishonest, she made herself tea and returned to reading the last of her ghost stories.

Perhaps it was because it was the wrong time of day for reading ghost stories, but she found herself unable to sink into its atmosphere and instead found herself thinking that the money that she had saved would not last for ever and that whatever happened here during the next few days, she must start thinking about the future. Letting the book sink on to her lap, she sat gazing vacantly at the window while the early winter twilight began to darken outside it. The room this evening felt cosy and friendly and she began to wish that she was not more or less committed to spending another night with the Graingers. But she did not want to hurt their feelings, if they wanted her to stay with them, and in any case she must go along to their cottage soon to see if they had come home and explain to them how she had locked herself out.

Actually, they might be home already. She got up, deciding that she might as well see if they were back before it got any darker, and walked along the short stretch of road to Rose Cottage.

But the door was locked, there were no lights in the windows and there was no car in the garage.

Returning home, she turned on the light, drew the curtains and, feeling that she would like a change from her ghosts, wondered if for once she could while away some time with a romance. Going to the bookcase, she picked out one of the paperbacks left behind, she supposed, by Nurse Wallace and settled down again by the fire. She opened the book and saw a piece of paper flutter out of it on to the floor.

She picked it up. There were only a few words written on it. "Please keep these. I've finished with them."

There was no signature, but the writing was the upright, forceful, rather spiky handwriting of the letter taken from Edgar Frensham's safe, shown to her briefly by Superintendent Barr.

She felt a surge of excitement. But to begin with she was not sure what it meant except that if these paperbacks had been given to Nurse Wallace by the writer of the letters in the safe, she must know who the writer was. Then another thought followed this. The writer must be someone within the small circle of people here whom Nurse Wallace knew. And there were not many women in that circle, Isobel Neville, Angela Bird, Liz Grainger. But the writing was quite unlike the writing of the receipt that Isobel Neville had given Charlotte, and it seemed to her impossible to imagine Mrs. Grainger carrying on a passionate love affair with Edgar Frensham. So that left Angela Bird. Called Birdie by the Graingers. B. And she was an artist. The specimen of her handwriting that she had given Mr. Barr might be quite unlike that of the letters in the safe, but might she not be able to disguise her writing at will with the skill of an artist, making it large or small, simple or ornate, upright or sloping, just as she chose? And had Charlotte ever quite believed in Angela Bird's antipathy to Edgar Frensham?

She sat staring at the paper in her hand as if it could tell her something more that she had missed. She knew that there were various things that she could do. She could get in touch with Mr. Barr and tell him what she had discovered. Or perhaps first she might telephone Nurse Wallace at the White Horse Hotel to ask her who had given her the paperbacks. Or she might telephone Timothy Royle and show him this piece of paper and explain how she had found it.

That was what she wanted to do. But would he be at the hotel now, and if not, how could she find him? In fact, it was obvious that she ought to get in touch with the police. Reluctantly she stood up, reaching for her handbag and tucking the paper inside it.

As she did so, she heard the squeak of the gate, footsteps on the path and the rattle of the door-knocker.

She opened the door. It was Angela Bird who stood there. For once she was not in her black and white outfit, but in the clothes, Charlotte supposed, in which she went to her work in the hospital, a brown tweed overcoat, brown walking-shoes and a small, dark red knitted cap. She looked older to Charlotte and plainer and less impressive than she ever had before. Her face was very white. Behind her the rain was a misty curtain, shimmering here and there where raindrops caught the light from the open door.

"May I come in?" she said. "An awful thing's happened. You'd better know about it."

She spoke jerkily and a little breathlessly and did not wait for Charlotte to ask her in, but stalked straight forward into the room. She pulled off her cap as she did so and shook back her short, dark hair.

"No one knows how it happened, but someone got into her room and stabbed Isobel," she said. "She's dead."

"Dead—in the hospital—killed?" Charlotte said blankly.

Angela Bird flung herself down in a chair. She took off her gloves and unbuttoned her overcoat. All her movements were jerky with nervous tension.

"There was supposed to be a policeman on duty, waiting for her to be able to talk," she said. "But she was under sedation and he'd been told there was no chance of her waking up for some hours, so he'd given himself a bit of a rest. And there were nurses about, but it was visiting-hours and there were lots of people coming and going and she was doing fine, so no one was keeping an eye on her. And someone got into her room and stuck a knife into her. It was left there in the wound, a common kitchen knife. And they've taken Mrs. Grainger to the police station for questioning."

"Mrs. Grainger!" Charlotte said incredulously. "But that's fantastic."

"Not as fantastic as it sounds," Miss Bird said. "She was seen leaving the hospital, carrying a big bunch of flowers, and when she was questioned, she said she'd come to bring the flowers to Isobel, but that she'd been told she wasn't allowed visitors, so she was leaving again, taking the flowers with her. But she couldn't describe the person who'd told her visitors weren't allowed, and the police couldn't find anyone who remembered speaking to her. And the knife could easily have been hidden in the bunch of flowers. And she had some story about having spoken to Beatrice Wallace to see if she'd look after Isobel when she came out of hospital, and Beatrice was quite willing and Mrs. Grainger wanted to tell Isobel at once, so that she needn't worry."

"That's right," Charlotte said. "That's what she said she was going to do. I saw her at lunch and she said she was going to the hospital."

"Well, the police don't think much of the story. It's obvious, you see, that if she had been seen by anyone when she was going in, she needn't have gone ahead with the murder, she could simply have said she'd come to bring the flowers."

"But what possible motive could she have had for killing Mrs. Neville?" Charlotte demanded. "It could only have meant that she'd something to do with Mr. Frensham's murder, and that just isn't possible."

"How d'you know? How d'you know what he'd been doing to her and her husband? What he'd been holding over them? Perhaps how he'd been bleeding them. I tell you, all kinds of people could have a motive for killing Edgar."

"How you hated him, didn't you?" Charlotte said. She hesitated and went on, "Or didn't you?"

The instant after she had spoken, she felt a shock of fear. For if what she had said had not been merely stupid, it had been dangerous. There could be danger in this room with her now, sitting in the chair facing her, tense and brooding.

Miss Bird's small, brilliant eyes widened, then the lids drooped over them and she seemed to withdraw into herself.

"I told you I was very attracted by him at first," she said in a low voice. "He could be very attractive when he chose. But my feeling didn't last long, and hate's rather a strong word for what I felt afterwards. I decided he was a rather contemptible person, that's all. I don't know what I've done to make you think what you do."

"You were in such a hurry to make us all think you disliked him intensely," Charlotte said, "and so couldn't possibly have written those letters in the safe."

"You've got it into your head I wrote them?"

"Didn't you?"

Miss Bird's eyelids had lifted again and she was regarding Charlotte with wonder.

"You know, you could get into trouble, saying things like that," she said. "It's lucky for you I don't take offence easily. How d'you explain the difference of handwriting?"

"It doesn't matter," Charlotte said. "I'm sure I was wrong."

"No, tell me." Miss Bird's voice was calm and friendly. It was her calm that made Charlotte feel frightened.

"It was just that I thought an artist could probably change her handwriting when she chose," she said. "And the letters are signed B. B for Birdie."

"Oh God, that awful name!" Miss Bird said. "No one but the Graingers ever calls me by it. I've tried to explain to them I don't like it, but they won't stop. I can assure you, if I was writing to a man I was in love with, I'd never use it. Anyway, why do you think those letters were written by anyone we know? They might have come from anywhere."

"They were written by someone Miss Wallace knows." Charlotte reached for her handbag and took out the paper that she had found in the paperback. "I found this in one of the books she left behind her."

She held the paper out to Miss Bird.

She looked at it frowningly. Then suddenly she crumpled it up, held a corner of it against a bar of the fire and let it catch alight. As it flared up, she tossed it on to the hearth, where it blazed for an instant, then collapsed in a little heap of ash. Looking up at Charlotte, she laughed.

"D'you know why I did that?" she asked. "Nurse Wallace's name is Beatrice and she was in love with Edgar and I've always been sorry for her, and that note could easily have been written by her and put into the book which she was meaning to give to someone else when she left here. Then she just forgot to do it. And if she's denying she wrote those letters, good luck to her. With her arm in plaster it'll be difficult to prove anything against her just yet."

"Do you believe she wrote the letters?" Charlotte asked, wondering with dismay how much it mattered that the scrap of evidence had been destroyed, but furious with herself for having let it happen.

"I think it's pretty likely, but even if she did, I'm sure she'd never murder anyone. I realize she could have wandered about the hospital, where she knows her way around, without attracting attention, but so could I. I work there. Why haven't you said that yet? Were you saving it up? And so could Dr. Maynard. There are plenty of possible suspects, once you start looking for them."

Charlotte nodded. "And there's one you haven't mentioned. Marcus Neville went to the hospital this afternoon. Ian Havershaw told me so."

"Did he? Now that *is* interesting." Miss Bird looked at Charlotte approvingly, as if she had just said something clever. "I'd settle for him as the murderer very willingly. But you've made up your mind it's me. I don't think I've ever roused such feelings in anyone before. I thought you rather liked me. Have you any other little surprises you're going to spring on me?"

Charlotte realized that she was being laughed at, and she disliked the feeling. If she had not, she might not have said what she did. "Whoever shot Mrs. Neville must have seen her car standing at my gate and I think you could have done that from your window."

Miss Bird came suddenly to her feet. At last she seemed angry. "You really have got it worked out, haven't you? I wonder how dangerous you are. Are you going to sell this idea of yours to the Superintendent? For the moment he likes Mrs. Grainger as a suspect and of course she could have seen the car from her window too, but perhaps you'll persuade him to switch to me. Only I don't think you believe half of what you're saying, or you wouldn't risk saying it to me here alone, with no one to stop me adding another murder to the list. No one saw me come here. I can make sure no one sees me leave. And I'm strong. I don't happen to have any weapon with me, but I think I could easily strangle you."

"I don't think either of us believes what we're saying," Charlotte said. "I suppose I was trying on my ideas for size.

Exploring possibilities. I can't stop thinking about it, and all kinds of queer things keep coming into my mind."

"Well, let me give you a piece of advice. Don't talk like this to anyone else, because it might be dangerous for you. It would dangerous now if I were the sort of person you half-think I am. But luckily for you, I'm not really violent."

Miss Bird went in long strides to the door.

Charlotte closed it after her, then returned to her chair and sat looking at the little heap of ash in the grate. She should never have let Miss Bird get her hands on the paper. She gave a sigh. The trouble was, she thought, she was not meant in the least for the kind of game that she was trying to play. The way that she had just been talking, what incredible folly. Miss Bird had been quite right to give her a warning. But what, at the end of it, was the truth about Miss Bird? Had she written those letters? Denial was so easy.

To make matters more disturbing, Charlotte had a feeling that a thought of some importance was dodging about at the edges of her mind. It had something to do with something that Miss Bird had said, but Charlotte could not grasp it. It seemed after all to be a shadow without substance. Instead of trying to pursue it—and find it dissolve when she thought that she had come close to it—it seemed more important to make up her mind what to do now that that scrap of paper, which she might have shown to the police, had been burnt and the possibility had been suggested to her that Nurse Wallace herself had written the few words on it. For if she had, of course she would deny it. Another easy denial, unless other specimens of her handwriting were available.

Charlotte gave a slight start. That was the thought that had been eluding her. Why had she not thought of it before? For certain, if the handwriting was Miss Bird's, there would be specimens of it in her office in the Infirmary.

The shadowy thought in Charlotte's mind became a little firmer in outline. She reached for her handbag to see what change she had in it, for she had just decided to go down the road to the telephone to try to make contact with Timothy Royle and see what he had to say about her idea. But she had only just opened her purse and seen with dismay that there were very few coins in it, when the gate squeaked and the door-knocker sounded. Putting her handbag down again, she went to open the door.

This time it was the Graingers. Both their faces had a curiously blank look of shock. They seemed to be looking at Charlotte questioningly, as if they were waiting for her to speak before either of them said anything. Although she held the door open for them to come in, neither of them moved.

"Won't you come in?" she said, realizing that the two of them were in the grip of some terrible embarrassment.

"Are you sure you want us to?" Mr. Grainger said more gruffly than usual.

"But why not?" Charlotte said.

"Don't you know what's happened?" Mrs. Grainger asked. Her voice was quavery.

"I've heard about Mrs. Neville," Charlotte said. "Miss Bird's been here. And she told me you were taken to the police-station for questioning. I expect the police are doing that with a lot of people. I'm sure it doesn't mean they suspect you of anything."

"Then why are you here?" Mrs. Grainger demanded. Her voice was suddenly loud. "We got home, we saw the house was dark, we saw your light here, we realized you didn't want to stay with us any more, and we thought, she believes this awful thing about us, she's afraid of us. So we came

here to find out if that's true. But it *is* true, isn't it? I know it
is. I'm very sensitive about things like that. I can usually
guess what other people are thinking. And I can see it in
your face that you think Ben and I are murderers."

"But I don't!" Charlotte was overcome by as much embarrassment as the Graingers. It was hardly fair of them,
she thought, to look her in the eye and demand that she
should judge them. "I only came here because I acciden-
tally locked myself out of your house. I forgot to take your
key with me when I went out in the morning, and when I
got back from Mattingley this afternoon there was no one in
yet, so I had to come here. I've only been waiting for you to
get home to ask if I can spend the night with you again. I
mean, if that wouldn't be a bother. I can manage all right if
you'd sooner be on your own."

Mrs. Grainger's face brightened at once. "Are you sure
of that, dear? It'd make us feel much better to have you
with us again, but don't come just to please us. I'm sorry we
weren't there when you got back in the afternoon."

"And d'you know why that was?" Mr. Grainger said
fiercely, as if he were accusing Charlotte of something.
"Those damned police didn't just question us, they didn't just
infer the most terrible things about Liz, who only went to the
hospital out of the kindness of her heart to see if she could
help cheer up poor Mrs. Neville by telling her everything
was fixed for her when she came out. They went to our shop
and searched it from top to bottom. We could have refused
to let them, but they said they'd only get a warrant. They
said they were looking for money. Money! Me and Liz!
Why, we've had to save for years to be able to put together
enough for the down-payment on the place. The rest's a
mortgage. Cash! Oh, my God! I was a clerk in a surveyor's
office most of my life, and if it was safe enough, it wasn't a
way to get rich. But we always wanted a small business of

our own, so we saved until we could manage it, and we were really happy when we came here, thinking we'd found just what we wanted. And now one foul thing happens after another—murder, suspicion and questioning, questioning. D'you know, they seem to think we robbed a bank. They seem to think Liz dressed up as a man and we wore false beards and all and got away with thousands. Everything's ruined for us. Liz will never get over it. She says the place has a bad atmosphere, and I shouldn't be surprised if she's right. She very often is. I think myself it stinks and the sooner we get out the better."

Mrs. Grainger began to give his shoulder tentative little pats, as if his anger had calmed her down.

"It's all right, love," she said. "I can be wrong sometimes, and I think this time I may have got a wee bit hysterical. It was seeing our windows dark and the light here that really upset me. I thought, Charlotte believes this thing about us and she's actually afraid of us. I couldn't bear that. But it makes me feel ever so much better now I know I was wrong. Come along, dear, let's go home and we'll have drinks and I'll put the supper on. I got some frozen prawn curry and rice in town, so I've only got to hot it up."

"Aren't the police going to search your cottage?" Charlotte asked.

"They may yet," Mr. Grainger answered. "But while they were talking to us a telephone call came through for that Superintendent and suddenly they didn't want us any more. In any case, I thought, they didn't seem to think we'd keep a lot of money where we lived, we'd hide it somewhere else. Only it happens they're wrong. If ever I lay my hands on a big sum of money, after this experience, I'm not going to hide it anywhere. I'm going to spend it. I'm going to feel rich and grand, even if it's only for a few days, before they arrest me—ha, ha!"

He suddenly began to shake with helpless laughter, the crowing laughter of nervous strain. Tears ran down his cheeks. His wife went on giving him consoling little pats.

"Of course, it *is* funny when you come to think of it," she said. "Me and Ben! Now let's go along. Get your coat and come with us, dear."

Charlotte put on her jacket, picked up her handbag, switched off the fire and the light and went with them.

Half-way to their cottage she stood still.

"Do you mind if I make a telephone call?" she said.

"Of course not. Go ahead, dear," Mrs. Grainger said. "It's such a nuisance there are no telephones in the cottages. But Ben had better go along with you. You haven't got a torch, have you?"

Charlotte had forgotten her torch. The one that the Graingers had brought with them carved a pale shaft of light through the drifting rain. It was very dark. She had also forgotten a head-scarf. In a moment her hair started to feel cold and clammy.

"It's all right, I can manage," she said.

"Then take the torch, dear," Mrs. Grainger said kindly as they reached the gate of Rose Cottage. "We don't need it now. And we'll expect you back in a few minutes."

She and her husband turned in at their gate. Charlotte muttered thanks for the torch and set off rapidly towards the telephone box on the edge of the village.

Trotting along the dark, miry road, she realized almost at once that she had been scared of the Graingers. The truth was, she was in a mood to be scared of her own shadow. Violence that might emerge from anywhere felt very close to her. It had been close to her, of course, on her first evening here, though she had not known it. What would have happened to her, she wondered, if she had arrived at Brickett's Farm a few minutes earlier, when murder was actually

being done? Would she have emerged alive? It seemed unlikely. She had survived by the narrowest of squeaks. And
how often could you be lucky when your mind had started
ticking over and you had found yourself understanding certain things that you had wholly misinterpreted earlier?

It had happened to her while the Graingers had been
with her. Certain things had come back to her with a meaning that she had not thought of giving them at the time.
Rather simple things. For instance, the fact that Nurse Wallace, with her right arm in plaster, could not have shot Mrs.
Neville unless she was left-handed. As perhaps she was. No
one, so far as Charlotte knew, had looked into that question. And it was the same with the letters. Unless she was
left-handed, her handwriting could not be tested until her
right wrist had recovered. And all of a sudden, thinking of
this, Charlotte had remembered a slim left hand being withdrawn from a glove, with a wedding-ring on one finger . . .

It was lucky that she had the torch, for the light in the
telephone box that should have come on when she entered
it, was out of order. However, there was a tattered directory
there and turning on the beam of the torch on to it, she
found the number of the White Horse Hotel. She took the
necessary coins out of her handbag and dialled. The ringing
tone seemed to go on and on for an endless time before a
voice of extreme indifference answered, asking in what
sounded like the middle of a yawn what he could do for her.
Charlotte dropped the money into the slot and replied that
she wanted to speak to Mr. Royle. She was told to hold on,
then silence descended, broken only by little pips and
squeaks.

Standing there waiting, she explored the telephone box
with the torch and saw it stated on the wall, written in the
most blood-red of lipsticks, that Linda loved Kevin. Someone else had written, "Wales forever!" As Wales was a long
way away, it seemed a strange thing to see, but perhaps a

Welsh football team had come to Mattingley on some occasion. There were also a number of obscene words, not embedded in sentences of any kind, but mere exclamations, it seemed, of an inarticulate sense of frustration. Then amongst all the other scribbles, Charlotte read that Linda loved Winston. She was wondering whether it was Kevin or Winston who reigned supreme in Linda's heart at the moment when a voice in her ear said, "Royle speaking."

"It's Charlotte," she said. "Listen and please don't interrupt. I'm in the public telephone box out here and we'll get cut off if I don't hurry. It's about the woman who wrote the letters to Edgar Frensham. It was Mrs. Neville. There was never anyone else. And I put people astray because I didn't understand something I saw. As a matter of fact, I don't think I ever told you anything about it, because it didn't seem awfully important, though I remember I told the police. But they didn't understand it any more than I did. You see, when I gave Mrs. Neville the rent for the cottage, I asked for a receipt and she got some paper and started taking off her left glove to write, then suddenly she jerked it on again and took off her right glove and scribbled a few words. And I thought she'd pulled on her left glove because she didn't want me to see her wedding-ring, when she was claiming to be Miss Sharples. But that wasn't why she did it at all. The truth is, she was going to write that receipt with her left hand, because she's left-handed, and if she'd done that, she would have written it in the same handwriting as the letters in the safe. But she didn't want anyone to know she'd written them. She meant to disappear with the money from the safe and she wanted people to think there was another woman in the case. And most left-handed people can write with their right hands after a fashion, because that's how they're taught at school, even though the writing is never as good as what they can do with their left—"

"In God's name," Timothy Royle interrupted, "why didn't you tell me this before? It's the most important thing—"

The line went dead. The money that Charlotte had put into the coin box had run out.

She groped feverishly in her handbag, but only found pence and halfpence and nothing that she could use in the telephone. Standing there helplessly, she felt as frustrated as ever the unfortunate could have been who had scribbled obscenely on the walls. Then she stepped out of the box and set off at a trot along the road to Rose Cottage.

Mrs. Grainger opened the door to her. A spicy smell of curry was wafted out to her.

"Ah, there you are," she said. "Come in and get warm. And Ben will give you a drink. Supper will soon be ready."

"Please," Charlotte said, "can I borrow ten p? I was in the middle of an important call and we got cut off and I found I hadn't any change to get through again. And I hadn't said half of what I meant to say."

"Of course," Mrs. Grainger replied. She turned to her husband. "Ben, have you got ten p? Charlotte didn't manage to finish her call."

He felt in a pocket and brought out a handful of change, then insisted that she should take twenty pence in case she got cut off again. Thanking him breathlessly, she went hurrying off down the road again, with her hair now sticking wetly to her scalp and cold drops beginning to trickle down inside the collar of her coat.

But her haste was useless. When the telephone started to ring again in the White Horse Hotel and the voice of utter indifference at last answered her and she asked for Mr. Royle once more, she was told that he had just left the hotel and had left no message about when he would be back.

CHAPTER TEN

Back in the Graingers' cottage, she was sent upstairs by Mrs. Grainger to give her hair a good rub with a towel, then she drank the very sweet sherry they gave her. But before she sat down by the log fire that they had lighted, and although she knew that Mr. Grainger was watching her, she went to the window, parted the curtains a little and peered out. There was no question about it, if a car had been standing at her gate, it could have been seen from here.

As she let the curtains fall back into place, she found Mr. Grainger watching her with a sardonic smile.

"Yes, I know what's on your mind and I might have done it, mightn't I?" he said. "But I'd have had to be pretty nippy. Her car stops at your gate, I see it, I see her get out, I see her walk up to your door, and I rush to get my gun, dash out in the dark and take a pot shot at her. And it's just my luck I've seen her arrive, because I don't usually stand watching at that window all day. All right, call the police and tell them you've got proof Liz and I are murderers."

He tried to make it sound as if he were joking, but he was very much on edge.

"I'm sure you aren't," Charlotte said, "but I was wondering if by any chance you saw the car pass."

"We didn't. We'd drawn our curtains before the trouble began. So if by any chance she went next door to visit Miss Bird and left her car outside while she went in to have a talk, we'd have known nothing about it. But, of course, you've only our word for that. If we'd seen the car there, I'd have had time to go and get my gun and do the dirty deed, shouldn't I? Sounds as if I'm trying to put a noose round my neck."

"Only if that's how it happened, you'd have shot her before she got back into her car, wouldn't you?" Charlotte said. "Because you couldn't have known she was only going to drive a hundred yards or so down the road and come to see me."

The nervous irony went out of his smile. It broadened into one of pleased good nature.

"Damn it, you're right! Liz!" He raised his voice. "Liz, did you hear that? Charlotte has just proved we couldn't have murdered Mrs. Neville. Oh—but—" His face fell. "Suppose it was us she came to visit. Suppose she told us she was going on to see you. In that case, there'd have been time for everything."

"You'd have been taking quite a risk, wouldn't you, if her car had been standing outside your gate for any time? Miss Bird or I might have seen it there, and so might anyone else who passed. You couldn't have been sure it hadn't been noticed and questions wouldn't be asked straight away."

He gave a gleeful little crow of laughter.

"Liz—Liz, did you hear that? This girl's really proving we're innocent."

"Well, of course we are," Mrs. Grainger answered from the kitchen. "Now I'm going to dish up. I hope you're hungry."

She came in, carrying bowls of curry and rice.

"Come along, finish your drinks and sit down," she said. "My goodness, I'm tired. Being questioned like that, it was terrible—" She gave a violent start. The door-knocker had just sounded. "No!" she cried, pressing her hands to her temples. "No, that can't be the police! I can't talk to them again! I can't, I won't!"

Mr. Grainger went to the door. It was not a policeman who stood there, but Timothy Royle. In the road outside the gate was a taxi.

"I'm sorry to bust in on you like this," he said, "but I've come to collect Miss Cambrey. She and I have got to talk to Mr. Barr. I think the sooner we see him, the better."

"But she's had nothing to eat," Mrs. Grainger protested, recovering quickly from her moment of frenzy. "We were only just sitting down to supper. Won't you come in and join us, Mr. Royle? There's plenty for everyone."

"I've got a taxi waiting," he said. "I think it would be best if we went at once."

Charlotte swallowed the rest of her sherry, then wished that she had not, for it seemed to help in bringing on a slight nausea as she went out to the taxi with Royle. The nausea, she knew, was only apprehension, excitement.

In the taxi she asked, "Are we really going to see Mr. Barr?"

"Of course," Royle said.

"I tried to telephone you again when we were cut off," she said, "but I was told you'd gone out."

"I went straight off to look for a taxi," he said. "I wanted to collect you before you did any more talking to anyone else. I didn't want you confiding in the murderer."

"Then d'you know who he is? Did what I told you tell you who he is?"

"It helped. Yes, decidedly it helped."

"I don't understand it myself," she said. "I understand a lot of bits and pieces, but I can't put them all together."

"Well, don't worry. I think we'll be able to do that between us." He smiled at her and it was such a kindly smile, so individual and somehow not quite like anyone else's, that she wondered how she could ever have thought him nondescript. "Don't look so frightened," he said. "We're near the end of this thing."

She nodded, trusting him. It gave her a comforting feeling that matters had been taken out of her hands. That was an immense relief. Taking responsibility, she thought, was something of which she had had more than enough. She had tried to do it for Dick's sake, but it had turned out to be too much for her. Or had she perhaps taken it more successfully than she had realized? Had she achieved more than she knew? Leaning back in the jolting taxi, she felt that she did not care much where it was taking her, to the police station, or on and on through the darkness in the curiously calming company of the man beside her. What did it matter?

However, it did take them to the police station. Royle told the desk sergeant that he had something of importance to say to Superintendent Barr. The sergeant said that he thought Mr. Barr had gone home, but it turned out, after some telephoning, that he was merely about to do so. When Charlotte and Royle were shown into his office, it was still filled with his immense presence, though he had on an overcoat and a tweed hat, which looked so small, perched on top of his big head, that it seemed he must absent-mindedly have helped himself to one that belonged to somebody else.

He removed it, but did not take off his coat when Charlotte and Royle came in. Sitting down in the chair behind his desk, he said, "Yes?" on a clear note of irritation which told them that what they had to say had better be of importance, for his home waited for him, drinks, a comfortable chair, a comfortable wife and a quiet evening ahead of him.

Charlotte and Royle took chairs facing him across the desk.

"Miss Cambrey has something to tell you about Mrs.

Neville that I think you ought to know," Royle said. "Go on, Charlotte, tell him."

It was less clear to her now than when she had spoken to Royle on the telephone, but with some hesitation she told Mr. Barr what she believed about the gesture of Isobel Neville's when she had started to take off her left glove, then jerked it on again. She also told him about the note that she had found in Nurse Wallace's paperback and she added, "And those letters were signed with a B. That could have stood for Belle, short for Isobel, which may have been what Mr. Frensham called her."

Mr. Barr began slowly to unbutton his overcoat, as if he were preparing to stay for some time.

"I see, yes," he said. "And where do you suppose that gets us?"

She looked at Royle, waiting for him to take over.

"Well, if you don't mind me beginning at the beginning," he said, "and telling you how I think things happened, it might save time. You can pick it to pieces afterwards. We're agreed, aren't we, that Frensham had been in gaol more than once and that he'd been brought here by his step-mother who hoped to stop him going on with that sort of life. And as far as she knew, all was well until he installed a safe in the house. That scared her because she was afraid it meant he was up to his old tricks, using his respectable life here as a cover. So I was called in to watch him and find out what he was really up to. I was to come to see her on Sunday morning, because Frensham would have been out playing golf and Miss Sharples would have been at church. But he was murdered before I could even get started, so I wasn't much help, but we can be pretty certain he was involved in that bank robbery for which Miss Cambrey's brother was convicted. It was Frensham's evidence that convicted him, together with a not-very-certain identification from one of the bank tellers. Frensham started a scuffle in the doorway while the two men with the money got away, and it was just Cambrey's bad luck that he was the one Frensham picked on to have the fight with. Then the money was brought here to Brickett's Farm and stowed in the new safe, waiting until it would be fairly safe to distribute it. There may have been more money there from other robberies. It's unlikely Frensham stayed honest all the time he was here. Do you agree with me so far?"

Mr. Barr nodded. "We know all this, or we're ready to think that's how it was," he said.

"Of course. I'm just laying a foundation," Royle replied. "Well, what I think happened on Saturday was this. A time had been agreed on when the proceeds of the robberies were to be split among the people involved, but Frensham didn't want to split with anybody. He wanted the lot for himself. He was probably dead tired of the dull life he was leading here and being bossed by his stepmother. What he intended was to disappear, faking a suicide. If he hadn't been stopped, you'd have got that suicide letter through the post, and you'd have found his car on the edge of a cliff or some such place, and you'd have supposed he'd thrown himself over. Incidentally, that's why he didn't mind letting Beech Cottage to someone with the name of Cambrey. He wasn't going to be around to see what she got up to."

Mr. Barr nodded again. "We'd worked that out too."

"Still, he made a number of mistakes, didn't he?" Royle went on. "To begin with—that letter. You never found it convincing, did you? It wasn't a clever letter. Too carefully composed, not nearly desperate enough. Then he wanted to take his mistress with him. Their scheme was that she should come to the house in her car, stow the money in it and drive off with him following her in his car, which he was going to leave on that cliff-top. Then he'd get into hers, so that they could drive on together to their destination, wherever that was. Before she came he'd switched off the chair-lift so that Mrs. Frensham couldn't come down and interrupt them in the middle of packing the money into the car—and it was Miss Sharples' day off. They had the house to themselves. And they'd put the money in the car and the luggage they were taking with them, leaving the front door open as they went in and out, when someone came in quietly and saw what they were doing. Doing what he'd probably been expecting and been prepared for. He was prepared to do murder, wasn't he? He'd brought a gun with him."

"Marcus Neville?" Mr. Barr suggested.

"No, Ian Havershaw."

"How d'you make that out?"

"I'm coming to that. For the moment let's just suppose I'm right about him. Something had made him suspicious, perhaps something Mrs. Neville had said to him, or perhaps, living next door to her, he'd seen her packing some luggage into a car when she hadn't said anything to him about going away. At any rate, he thought, it was time for him to investigate what was going on. So he walked across the fields to Brickett's, found the door open and went in and realized how he and Neville were being double-crossed."

"He and Neville?" Mr. Barr said. "They were in it together?"

"Of course. They were the two men who got away with the money from the bank. And I don't think either of them was in love with Mrs. Neville. That was just cover. Well, Havershaw didn't waste any time. He shot Frensham and perhaps he would have shot Mrs. Neville too if it hadn't happened that Miss Cambrey rang the doorbell at just that moment."

Charlotte drew her breath in sharply. "It really *was* then?"

"Oh yes, you were practically in at the kill. The murderer was still in the drawing-room with Frensham's body. Mrs. Neville answered the door. And when you paid the rent and asked for a receipt she wrote it with her right hand, because she didn't want to be identified with the woman who'd written the letters in the safe. He'd shut the door on them, so that she couldn't get at them. I imagine he wanted to have some kind of hold over her, and the way she threatened him gave away that she knew all about his criminal activities."

"But mightn't we have suspected something of all this if she'd disappeared at the same time as he did?" Mr. Barr asked.

"She didn't mean to disappear," Royle answered. "If there'd been no murder she'd have driven off with Frensham, dropped him wherever he was going, perhaps stayed a little while, but come back within two or three days. Then soon afterwards she'd have come up with a good reason for leaving Mattingley, and the two of them would have faded out together. We could have arrived at all this far sooner if we hadn't been more or less convinced there was another woman in the case."

"I'm sorry, it's my fault," Charlotte said humbly. "But I thought there was another woman, and I thought of Miss Bird and Nurse Wallace and even, just vaguely, Mrs. Grainger."

"You told us what you saw," Superintendent Barr said. "It wasn't your fault that we misinterpreted it as well as you." He looked back at Royle. "What happened next? At the moment you've got Mrs. Neville in the house with the murderer. What did she do?"

"Left it as fast as she could," Royle answered. "Shut the

door after Miss Cambrey, then immediately opened it again, went running out to the car and drove away before the murderer even realized what she meant to do. Drove off to that place to which she'd meant to go with Frensham. I don't know where it was, but if you ever find it, that's where you'll find the money. And she stayed holed up there till she'd had time to think. Then she began to think she'd done a rather stupid thing. She didn't want to remain a fugitive for the rest of her days. It would have been different if she'd been with Frensham, but alone, hunted by Neville and Havershaw as well as the police, she felt she was in far too much danger to be comfortable. So she got in touch with her husband—"

"Why him?" Barr interrupted. "Why not Havershaw?"

"For a very simple reason. Havershaw had no telephone in that cottage of his, but Neville had one in London. So she telephoned him and offered a deal. If he'd obliterate all signs of her having been the woman who wrote the letters, she'd tell him and Havershaw where the money was and share it with them. So Neville came down here and searched her cottage for every scrap of writing she'd done with her left hand. Miss Cambrey and I caught him at it. When he let us into the cottage we could see he'd been searching for something, though we didn't know what. But that's what I think you'll find it was. And meanwhile Mrs. Neville was also getting rid of traces of her normal writing. She got rid of her old diary and bought a brand new one, which, you may remember, hadn't a single entry in it when you found her after she'd been shot in Miss Cambrey's doorway."

"So now we've got around to that," Mr. Barr said. "But just why did she go there? And why do you say it was Havershaw who shot her, not Neville?"

"Isn't it plain she was shot by someone in her own car?" Royle said. "One or two other people, Miss Bird or the

Graingers, for instance, might have seen the car in the road, but they could hardly have moved fast enough to have got hold of a gun and shot her by the time Miss Cambrey opened her door to her. No, her murderer was sitting in the car with her. She probably expected him to go in with her and see Miss Cambrey. Then, as soon as he'd shot her, he ran off down the road to his own cottage. I heard running footsteps, but the bus from Mattingley went by just then and drowned the sound of them. And I thought it was more important to go in to help Miss Cambrey than to try chasing him. But I don't think it was Neville. He was staying at the White Horse Hotel, and she'd have had to get in touch with him somehow if he was to come out with her, and when he ran off there'd have been nowhere for him to go but to Havershaw. Why should he have chosen a place for the murder from which it would be so difficult for him to get away? It's much more complicated than if she simply went back to her own cottage, went in to see Havershaw and was persuaded by him to go and see Miss Cambrey?"

"But why did she do that?" Charlotte asked. "I still don't understand that."

"I think he persuaded her to come to you to check up that no one suspected her of having written the letters. You were the person to whom she'd given the misleading receipt. You were the person who was likely to know what had become of it. That's what he made her think, anyway. He didn't want to shoot her in his own house and have to get rid of the body. A mysterious shot out of the darkness as she stood on your door-step was quite a convenient way of disposing of her. A number of other people could be suspected. The evidence didn't point straight at him. Of course, he'd got out of her by then where the money was, or he wouldn't have thought of killing her. And I shouldn't much like to be Neville at the moment, because I think Havershaw wants it all to himself. I'm not telling you a story about honour among thieves."

"But it was Neville who went to see her this afternoon in the hospital," Charlotte said. "Ian drove me home after lunch and he said he'd agreed to Neville being the one who should try to see her."

"Oh, he did, did he?" Royle said. "Making sure that Neville, in his rather conspicuous red velvet suit, had gone in before he himself went in there later."

"He took me to his cottage and gave me his manuscript to read," Charlotte went on. "As a matter of fact, I thought there was something a bit funny about it, because the paper was so yellow, it looked as if it had been written a good while ago. I'm beginning to wonder if he's actually the person who wrote it at all."

"Perhaps not," Royle said. "Perhaps he got it from somebody else. He was posing here as a writer while he waited for the distribution of the money, so he may have felt it was safer to have some protective colouring." He turned back to Mr. Barr. "I think if you want to know where the money is, you've only to keep an eye on Havershaw."

Mr. Barr gave one of his bleak little smiles. For the first time he looked as if he were enjoying the conversation.

"As it happens, we know where the money is," he said. "It's in the Brighton police-station. We had a telephone call about it while I was interrogating the Graingers. The place where Frensham intended to hole up, at least temporarily, was a flat there, which he rented some weeks ago. Then when he didn't arrive at the time he had said he would and only a woman came and went rather mysteriously, the caretaker decided to see that all was well and went in and found a suitcase bulging with money. The description of the woman fitted the one the Brighton police and other police forces have had from us, and they got in touch with us this afternoon. The flat is under observation and we're waiting to see who turns up to collect the money."

Royle stared at him for a moment, then began to laugh.

"So I needn't have told you all this," he said. "You knew it all along. The professional is always ahead of the amateur."

"Not at all, not at all," Mr. Barr said generously. "You've filled in a lot of gaps very usefully. Explained a number of things we didn't understand. I'm most grateful for your help. And I think, acting on that hint you dropped, we'll keep a rather careful eye on Mr. Neville, to see that he comes to no harm. I've a feeling he'll end up a very useful witness. He'll crack under questioning. Besides, if you're right that he didn't commit either murder, he'll see it's to his own advantage to tell what he knows. He's a type I'm well acquainted with. We'll be able to use him."

That, in fact, was how it fell out. The murders had frightened Marcus Neville deeply, and once he began to talk, as Mr. Barr later told Charlotte, it was hard to stop him. Ian Havershaw, on the other hand, closed his lips over his large teeth and refused to say anything at all, except to demand to see a solicitor. His solicitor presumably advised continued silence, for Ian remained mute. It made Mr. Barr uneasy, for except for what Neville was only too eager to say, there was not much solid evidence against him.

"But you needn't worry any more," Timothy Royle said to Charlotte. "Your brother will be given a pardon. The law moves horribly slowly and it may take a little time, but at least I should say there's a chance that he'll get some kind of compensation. All the same, I think it would be a good idea if I put you in touch with a really good solicitor when we get back to London."

They were on their way up to Brickett's Farm as he said

it. Charlotte wanted to tell Mrs. Frensham that she was leaving and to hand over to her the keys of Beech Cottage. She had said good-bye to Miss Bird and the Graingers, had given Mrs. Grainger what remained in her refrigerator, had packed her belongings and a taxi had been ordered. It was a cold morning, with the blueness of the sky showing only faintly through a low-lying mist.

"I'm going to see you in London, am I?" she said.

"Unless you've anything against it," he answered.

"Only those five children."

He put an arm round her shoulders. "Oh come, you never believed in them for a moment, did you?"

"Not exactly, no."

"But why not, that's what I don't understand. What did I say wrong?"

"Well, *five*. It was overdoing things. If you'd said one, or twins, or even triplets, I might have believed you, but five was excessive. Then when I questioned you about them, you were very vague. You forgot their names. And there's something about you that isn't specially paternal. Perhaps you don't look harassed enough. Have you got a wife?"

"Not even one."

"What I don't understand," she said, "is why you put on the act. What made you do it?"

"It was an impulse when I saw you in the train. I knew who you were and what you'd been through, and you looked so withdrawn and forlorn I thought if I made an ordinary pass I'd get nowhere with you. And I wanted to talk to you, and that only partly for professional reasons. So I thought I could present myself to you as a man wrapped up in his own family, even a sort of father-figure whom you might feel like confiding in."

She gave a little giggle. "I think the truth is, you just like playing parts."

"Yes, that's true. I like having different personalities for different jobs. I think it's because I lead such an anonymous kind of life. I generally have to merge into the background. So something a little more colourful in my own imagination helps to keep me going. I don't tell a great many lies in the ordinary way."

"That's good."

"And in reality I should never want to have five children. I think the world is over-populated already."

"I agree absolutely."

"So we could meet in London, couldn't we?"

"If you want to."

They had reached the door of Brickett's Farm. Charlotte rang the bell. Miss Sharples opened the door to them.

"There now, we were only just talking about you, dear," she said. "Mrs. Frensham said she was sure you'd just go off, leaving everything in a mess, now you've got what you wanted, but I said no, she isn't like that, I said, you'll see she'll leave everything in order. But she said, how am I going to manage at my age now that I haven't got Mr. Edgar to look after the property, because he always did that well, whatever he may have done otherwise. So I said, why don't you sell up everything, dear, I said, and go into a home? With your money, I said, there's no reason you should have business worries and you could afford to go into some really nice place—"

"Emily!" a shrill old voice shouted from the drawing-room. "Who the devil are you chattering to out there? Who is it?"

Miss Sharples signalled to Charlotte and Royle to come in. She led them to the drawing-room. Mrs. Frensham, wearing her purple quilted dressing-gown and her diamond ear-rings, was in a chair with her aluminium crutches leaning against the arm of it. A rug had been put down on the cream-coloured carpet, hiding whatever had been left of the blood-stains.

"Oh, it's you," she said, her black eyes glaring at them fiercely. "What d'you want now?"

"I came to say good-bye and to bring you the keys of the cottage," Charlotte said.

"Oh, you're leaving? You're entitled to stay in the place for a month, if you want to," the old woman said. "That's in your agreement. I don't go back on agreements. You owe me three weeks' rent in any case."

"I'll send you a cheque," Charlotte said.

"Very well. Don't forget." Mrs. Frensham's gaze shifted to Timothy Royle. "If you think I went back on our agreement, young man, you can tell your employers I'll pay their fee up to today. You did what I engaged you to do, more or less, even if you took your time about it. And I don't believe in quibbling over trifles. That man Barr tells me you helped to clear up the mess. Mind you, I don't know what I'm going to do without Edgar to look after things for me. D'you know what that bloody woman Emily wants me to do? Go into a home, she says. Me! I'm going to die in my own bed, that's something I'm quite clear about. I suppose I can get an agent to look after things for me. He'll rook me, of course. Everyone thinks they can rook a woman of my age. Well, it doesn't matter if he does. I've no one to leave anything to now, and I've no special wish to leave it all to some bloody charity, though I suppose that's what I'll have to do in the end. I'm taking care of Emily, of course, and I'm leaving a bit to Ralph Maynard, because he's a really good man, whatever threats Edgar may have tried to frighten him with. He did frighten him, I'm afraid, because a doctor can't risk scandal, even if there's absolutely nothing to it. But except for those two, I'd like to die intestate. Only I shan't be here to watch the wrangle they'll all have over it, so I'll miss the fun. What a pity one can't have a sort of dress-rehearsal for one's death, isn't it, to see how everyone's going to behave? I'd really enjoy that. But I expect you think I'm a pretty bloody old woman, don't you?"

All at once, in the way that she had, she leant her head back against her cushions and closed her eyes. It was as if she was shutting them out of her consciousness and perhaps already out of her memory. In her long life the last few days had been only an incident. Perhaps she had known worse. In any case, the incident was closed.

Tip-toeing, Miss Sharples led them to the door.